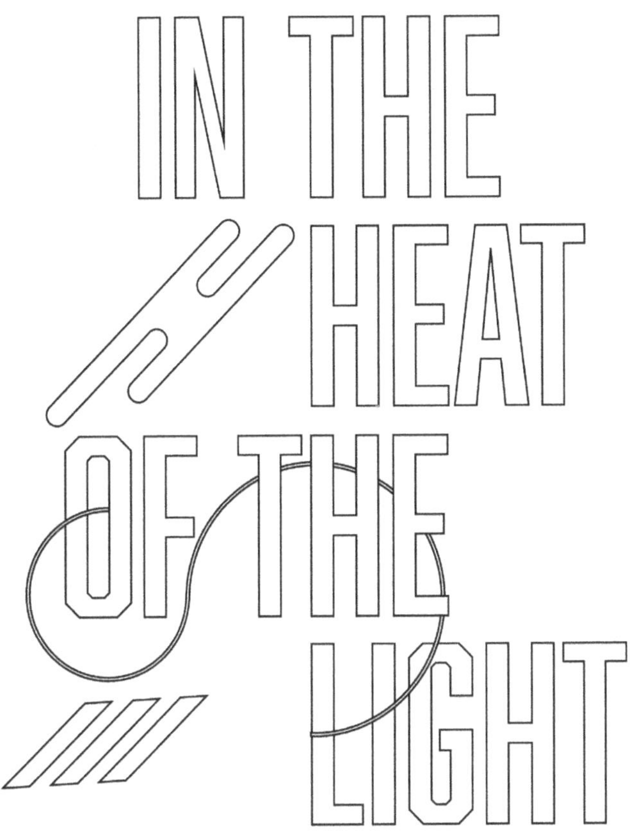

IN THE
HEAT
OF
THE
LIGHT

I0719732

IN THE HEAT OF THE LIGHT

STEPHEN KEARSE

KINDRED BOOKS

GREEN BAY, WISCONSIN

Published in the United States by Kindred Books, an imprint of Brain Mill Press.
Print ISBN 978-1-948559-29-4
EPUB ISBN 978-1-948559-32-4
MOBI ISBN 978-1-948559-30-0
PDF ISBN 978-1-948559-31-7

Break Up
Words and Music by Sean Garrett, Shondrae Crawford and Radric Davis
Copyright (c) 2009 SONGS OF UNIVERSAL, INC., TEAM S DOT PUBLISHING and UNKNOWN PUBLISHER
All Rights for TEAM S DOT PUBLISHING Administered by SONGS OF UNIVERSAL, INC.
All Rights Reserved   Used by Permission
Reprinted by Permission of Hal Leonard LLC

BREAK UP
Words and Music by RADRIC DAVIS, SEAN GARRETT and SHONDRAE CRAWFORD
© 2009 WC MUSIC CORP., RADRIC DAVIS PUBLISHING, LLC and CO-PUBLISHER(S)
All Rights on behalf of Itself and All rights on behalf of itself and RADRIC DAVIS PUBLISHING, LLC Administered by WC MUSIC CORP.
All Rights Reserved
Used By Permission of ALFRED MUSIC

Cover design by Felicia Penza.

www.brainmillpress.com

DEDICATED TO MAE FRANCIS HARRIS

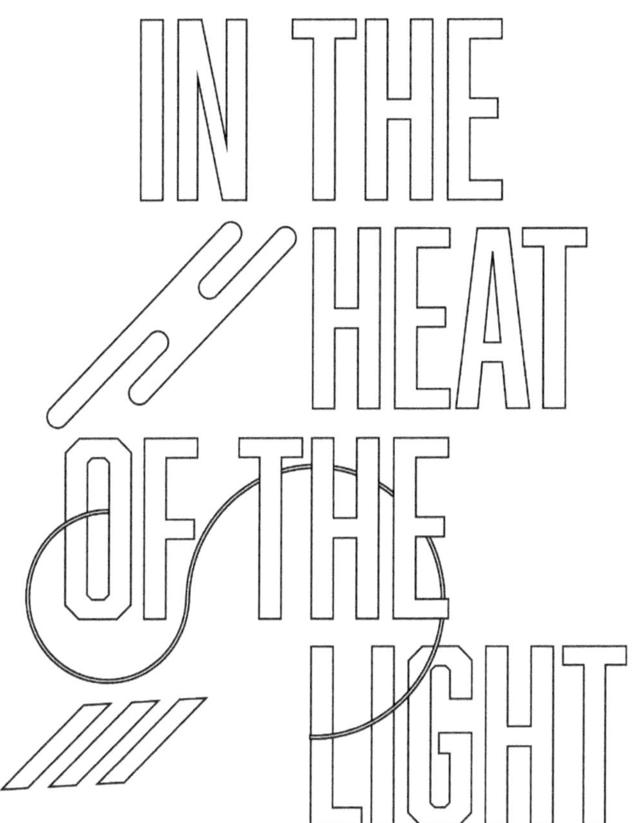
IN THE
HEAT
OF THE
LIGHT

JUNE

AVERAGE HIGH: 86°F

AVERAGE LOW: 68°F

CHAPTER 1
JUNE 14
8:52 A.M.
78°F

KAI WATCHED AS THEO BEGAN HIS RITUAL DANCE. First, he stepped out of his Honda Civic, sighing deeply as the humid Atlanta air swarmed around him. Next, he tipped his cap and mopped his brow—as usual, there was no sweat, but tradition is tradition. Finally, the waltz: sluggishly, he ambled up Kai's winding driveway, each step a marathon, each breath a pull from a toothpick-sized cigarette.

"You look like an asshole," Kai said when he reached the doorway.

Kai used to believe that all black people had a high tolerance for heat and humidity, or at least a willingness to adapt to it, but Theo had proved her wrong. His suffering was excruciating and singular. He'd lived in Atlanta for five years, and he'd resisted its weather each day. Today, his dumb ass stood before her in a maroon tank top, a burgundy Anaheim Ducks snapback, a gray hoodie, black skinny jeans, and black Vans. California boys were real knuckleheads.

Theo stepped inside, removing his cap and fanning himself. Kai kissed him and herded him into the kitchen. They eased into place at the dining table, sitting apart. The kitchen was the coolest room in the house. Kai's parents rarely cooked, so they filled the counters with potted plants. Theo liked to call it the Green Room, much to the annoyance of Kai's father, Mr. Forrester. He'd served time for selling marijuana, so he had no tolerance for references to weed. Kai had once looked up his sentence online and saw that he'd only served 30 days, but she never called him out on it or told Theo. She liked secrets.

"It's nine o'clock," Theo said. "Apollo and Zed should be here soon. Sol is working till seven."

"Cool. So what's the move for today?"

"I'm thinking we'll just lay low until it's time for the main event. I've got everything set up for tonight. Alibis, van, encrypted laptop, burners. All I need is gas."

"Are you sure about this?" Kai asked. "This isn't an ordinary tag."

"I'm not an ordinary nigga."

Kai rolled her eyes.

The doorbell rang. Kai jumped up and ran to the door, her curls bouncing in cadence with her strides. She returned with Apollo. "Today's the day, boss! You ready?" he asked, thumping Theo's shoulder with his heavy hands.

"I think so. Why aren't you sweating? It's hot as hell out there." Theo threw a light jab, targeting Apollo's stomach.

Apollo dodged. "Unlike you, I accept that I live in hell, so I dress accordingly." He slapped his thigh then goofily jumped in place, his nylon shorts swish-swishing around his knees.

Zed walked into the kitchen next. "Shut up, Apollo," she said. "You know you can only handle heat because you're Nigerian."

Kai sucked her teeth. "Zadie, you know Nigeria has snow-capped mountains, right?"

"That was good, but don't call me Zadie. It's Zed now," Zed said firmly.

"Zed, Zee, Zade," Theo joked. "When are you going to go by something that isn't Z-related? You're like the X-Men."

"Ai ai ai, back to business, people," Apollo interrupted. "Theo, you never answered my question. You *are* ready, right?"

"We should be asking you. You're the hacker," Theo countered.

"Don't give me that reverse psychology bullshit. This was your idea. Are you ready or not?"

Theo remained silent, his eyes shirking beneath the bill of his hat.

Kai knew Theo wanted her to chime in, but instead, she idly flicked the leaves on one of the kitchen plants. The plan was definitely going down, but she needed to hear Theo admit it to himself in front of everyone else, not just her. Some secrets were better out in the open.

"Yeah, I'm ready. I just need to get some gas first."

"Let's ride, then," said Zed.

They filed out of the house. Zed drove a black 2013 MINI Cooper, a graduation gift. Kai hated the tiny car. Something about its safety annoyed her. Whenever she rode with Zed, she played with the locks and plucked at her door handle, just to see if the car would somehow express disapproval; she felt it had that kind of vibe.

"I'm riding with Theo," she announced. No one seemed surprised. She moved Theo's windbreaker and overstuffed backpack to the back seat before climbing in. Theo started the engine, and they were greeted by KEY!, Theo's newest favorite rapper. Kai smiled to herself.

Theo used to pride himself on how much Atlanta rap he *didn't* listen to. He loved the disappointed looks people gave him when he told them he was listening to Kendrick Lamar and Suga Free and Vince Staples. But Atlanta music had gradually managed to slip past his defenses. He had grown to enjoy Lil Baby, Future, Young Thug, Father, and even Gucci Mane. He had fallen so far, Kai had begun to joke that he was about to start selling mixtapes outside of a Waffle House.

Theo slowly backed out of the driveway, lingering for Zed, who was parked in the street. Kai stared at the clock on the dash: 9:22 a.m. She regretted inviting everyone over so early. Zed's lights flashed and Theo pulled off, breezing past the stop sign at the end of Kai's block and racing toward the entrance to her subdivision. Kai didn't see Zed in the side mirror, but she knew she would appear soon. They played this game often: Zed always took the same route.

Plywood dream homes sped by as they zipped around the neighborhood's wide streets, dodging parked cars and frolicking children. No OUTLET signs stood like sentinels on the corners of the subdivision's multiple cul-de-sacs, intensifying the neighborhood's overwhelming blandness. When they reached the final stretch, Kai checked the side mirror again. No one was there. Zed usually wasn't this far behind. *Theo must have really floored it,* Kai thought.

As the neighborhood sign came into view, Kai pointed at the car parked next to it and laughed. Zed had floored it, not Theo. The car slowed to a crawl as Theo pulled past the MINI Cooper, throwing Zed and Apollo a smirk through the Civic's sealed passenger window.

"That was different," Theo lamented.

"Left," Kai instructed as they approached the main thoroughfare, Bethsaida Road.

"Where are we headed?" Theo asked, always reluctant to navigate without his GPS.

"Gas station," Kai answered coolly.

"Oh. Can we go to one that's kind of in the cut? A bunch of teens stopping to put gas in containers probably looks a little suspicious."

"For sure. The station I have in mind is pretty low-key," Kai assured him.

Minutes later, they pulled into the lot of a Shell on Old National Parkway. Theo groaned, but Kai knew he only recognized the street name from a 2 Chainz verse.

"This is not low-key. This street is world famous!"

"I think you mean World Star famous. I've seen armed robberies, assaults, fistfights, motorcycle races, and three-dollar ribs on this street. Everything is suspicious here. So, nothing is suspicious. It's perfect. Get the gas, fool."

Theo sucked his teeth and exited the car, firmly closing the door. Watching him, Kai laughed as he stepped in line and gripped the brim of his hat with both arms, wobbling in place. He was so shook.

With a false coolness, he exited the store, shoulders low and head high. Popping the trunk, he removed two 2-gallon gas containers. Kai wasn't surprised when he loudly sighed as he closed the trunk. He'd probably just realized he'd have to stay outside to fill up the car.

Kai scrolled through Twitter. Her timeline wasn't active, but the activity of the previous night was still available. Apollo had been watching anime again, and Zed had been forced to join him. She'd tweeted a string of annoyed rhetorical questions: "Why are their eyes so big? #anime." "Does everyone need a damn backstory? #anime." "Japanese voice actors are loud af. #anime."

Kai laughed. Zed must really like Apollo to be tolerating anime. She typically scoffed at all things she deemed "childish," and her scorn for childishness had only increased since they had graduated three weeks ago. Not only had her tweets suddenly become grammatically perfect, but when Zed and Kai hit up

Lenox Mall a week after graduation, Zed had sneered at all clothing that wasn't black, gray, or burgundy. "Women's colors," she'd called them. Just wait till she meets Apollo's mom, Kai had thought. Mrs. Aleyani dressed like every day was a festival. She had dresses in marigold, rose, amethyst, fuchsia, maroon, lily, saffron, and cerulean. Kai swore that simply looking at this extravagant woman could improve your color vocabulary.

"What's so funny?" Theo asked, getting back into the car.

"Just Twitter," Kai replied, noting Theo's soaked brow. The heat was already getting to him.

He started the engine and waved to Zed and Apollo, who were parked a few feet away. Zed's lights flashed in response, and moments later, they were on Old National, heading north toward Sol's Waffle House. Kai gazed out the window, listening to the click of the door lock. She had no illusions about the activity on Old National. She knew about the drugs, the stickups, the prostitution, the shuttered businesses—but it was home, and it annoyed her that Theo kept skittishly relocking the car door. He had been driving to this side of town for years, but he still treated it like some kind of postapocalyptic wasteland. *And* he still thought a locked car door could keep him from danger. Dumbass. Kai sighed as they approached World Changers Church.

Right on cue, Theo turned down the music and launched into his routine tirade against Creflo Dollar, the church's founder. "I hate that damn dome! I just don't get why people go there. He has 'dollar' in his name, and he has a fucking record company. He's like the P. Diddy of an alternate universe, except instead of selling Ciroc, he sells Jesus. He literally pimps Jesus! And look where his home base is. He makes money off black people and presents himself as our savior at the same damn time!"

Kai chuckled. Theo had said "at the same damn time." Even though he still had a settler's naive fears, he was steadily becoming an Atlantan. She could do without the rant, though—everybody pimps Jesus, to be honest.

A few minutes later, they pulled into the Waffle House parking lot. It was completely empty except for a bicycle. Waffle House was the premiere breakfast spot, but not at breakfast hours.

"Welcome to Waffle House!" shouted Sol's coworkers as Zed, Theo, Kai, and Apollo slid into a corner booth. Instinctively, they wiped their sections of the table before placing their phones on its surface. Waffle House served syrup on tap and on tabletops.

Sol emerged from the bathroom and immediately greeted them. "Ayyy, it's my favorite crew, the Celestials!" she announced to the empty restaurant. "And Apollo," she added.

"Solara, it's not my fault you were named after a shitty Toyota instead of a car people actually like," Apollo retorted, catching her shade and throwing his own. Sol blankly stared at him. She'd spent a year in juvenile, so insults, even ones that should have at least left a dent, simply bounced off her. *Apollo should have known better,* Kai thought. He'd probably sat on that comeback for months too. Damn shame. It was actually pretty clever.

"Need some water?" Sol asked, addressing the table, but looking at Apollo.

"Yeah, we'll take some," Kai told her, admiring Sol's audacity as she walked behind the counter, confident despite her frumpy uniform. Sol had always been honest, but juvie had amplified that honesty tenfold. Sol never talked about what happened while she was locked up, but it wasn't hard to guess. She had come back with chiseled arms, broad shoulders, muscular thighs, and an attitude to match. She could escalate situations as easily as she could flex a muscle. Yet she wasn't visibly intimidating. Far worse, her game was selective intimidation. She never wore her gun on her hip; she just brandished it whenever she wanted to shoot, which was often when Apollo was around.

Returning to the table, Sol smoothly issued four menus and four cups of ice-cold water from behind the counter. Kai chuckled as Apollo checked his for spit, frowning at her and Zed from across the table. Theo dutifully glanced over the menu, making Kai proud. He'd been raised on the gospel of Denny's, but the transition to Waffle House hadn't been difficult. Hot plates had nothing on good food.

"You got a minute?" Theo asked Sol.

"Nah, it's mad busy right now," she said, stepping back and extending her arm toward the vacant restaurant like a showgirl introducing a showcase on *The Price Is Right.*

The table laughed, settling in. "For real, though, is everything square for tonight? This ain't no regular fucking tag," Sol said, bending over and dropping her voice to a hush. All eyes fell onto Theo.

"Yeah, it's all good. We're picking up the van tonight as planned, Six Flags is closed all day for emergency parking lot repairs, the movies are still playing so we can get tickets, and McPherson is still in transition. I checked everything. Nothing can go wrong," Theo said.

"Right," Sol replied. "I hope y'all have better clothes, though. Nylon shorts, skinny jeans, coochie cutters, and a skirt aren't the right gear."

A wave of foolishness washed over the table, making Sol laugh. Kai knew Theo had forgotten something. He'd have to go all the way back to Marietta to get a change of clothes. She looked down, contemplating his wardrobe. It was more uncredited Odd Future member than criminal, but he could work it. As long as you had black skin, being a criminal didn't take too much work. Kai prayed he didn't say something stupid.

"We know that," Theo responded. "I'm just the driver, so I don't need to be on my cat burglar tip. Everybody else is going to go home and change, though."

"Sure," Sol said, skeptical.

"Anything else, Sergeant Sol?" Zed asked, waving the laminated menu. "I'm trying to go in."

"Yes," Sol said, standing up and returning to her full height, 70 inches. "Kai, buy a damn wig. I know you think everyone and their mama is going natural, but it's actually just you and a couple thousand Insta thots, so you natural hoes be standing out. Weave still reigns supreme. Trust me, I work night shift on Fridays." She removed her hat and pointed at her wavy, imported hair. She practiced what she preached.

Kai laughed and nodded. Sol took their menus and returned to the kitchen, announcing, "Four waffles, three hash browns, and one cup of surprisingly good coffee, coming right up!" Her announcement went unheard by her two coworkers who were smoking out front, but Sol probably didn't care. She was used to doing things herself.

CHAPTER 2
JUNE 14
12:40 P.M.
86°F

ROWS OF STYLISH FIBERGLASS HEADS PEERED DOWN at Apollo as he followed his friends through the beauty supply store, one of the many cacti of Riverdale, Georgia's strip mall desert. Zed led the way, evaluating wigs for Kai. "Too chic. Too fifties. Too boring. Too boy band," she chanted in cadence with her steps. Apollo quietly trailed behind Kai, wondering what she was thinking. Her natural hair journey, as he had learned to call it, had entailed an utter dismissal of beauty supply stores. He'd seen her YouTube videos declaring beauty supply stores as black women's final plantation. Returning to one after a three-year-long boycott must have been strange.

The prices seemed outrageous, but he wasn't sure if they actually were or if he just spent too much time on the internet. The last thing he had bought in a physical store that wasn't food or entertainment or electronics was condoms.

He was surprised that they weren't being followed. Beauty shops in Riverdale were notoriously hostile to black customers despite being sustained entirely by black money. A few years back, one store had even tried to implement a dress code: no sandals with socks, no do-rags, no bonnets, no sweatpants, no hats, no jerseys, no spaghetti straps, no A-shirts. It had stayed in business a whole two weeks before closing with a huge liquidation sale during which people bought the store's banned items in bank-breaking bulk.

Zed stopped abruptly, her eyes settling on a bright red wig of straight hair. "RiRi red, yaaas," she declared. "This is your look." Kai grimaced, looking back at Apollo and Theo for confirmation. They exchanged shrugs.

The crew made their way to the counter, where they were politely greeted by a bored Korean clerk. "Will you be purchasing anything else today?" the clerk asked as she rang up the wig, addressing them all. Apollo stared at the front door. "Are you sure?" the clerk insisted, facing Theo in particular. "We have bandanas…" she began. Apollo scowled. "They help with the heat," she finished.

"I'll pass," Theo responded, flashing a smile.

Exiting the store, Apollo turned to Kai. "Where to next?" Apollo checked his phone. 12:47. They had six hours until Sol got off work. Apollo wondered why in the hell they had met up so early.

"Let's go see Jerry," Zed suggested.

"Who's Jerry?" Apollo asked as he and Zed filed into her car.

"An old friend," Zed replied. She clicked her seat belt and started the engine. Apollo groaned. He hated mysteries. He hacked precisely because he thought there were too many mysteries in the world, too many black boxes, too many encrypted files, too many passwords.

His thoughts were drowned out by NPR, Zed's favorite station and the only one she ever tuned in to. "What is the legacy of Dwayne McDuffie?" the broadcaster asked. Apollo perked up, energized by a faint recognition of the name. His brow furrowed as the intro segment segued into an equally familiar symphonic music clip.

"Ughhh," Zed moaned. "More cartoon shit." She flicked off the radio, plunging Apollo into another chasm of mystery.

They rode in silence as Kai and Theo led them south down Highway 85. The car lurched to the right when Zed hit a left turn too quickly. "Sorry!" she shrieked. They continued down Church Street, passing homes and a school, eventually turning left down Evans Road, a winding side street. Zed slowed as they pulled into a church parking lot.

"Ohhh, Dwayne McDuffie basically invented the Justice League cartoon," Apollo said with awe, looking up from his phone, mouth agape.

"And Static Shock," Zed said matter-of-factly, removing her seat belt and clicking the trunk open. Apollo joined her outside of the vehicle, where she stood with a paint-splattered beige tote bag. He loved this chick.

Finished with the mystery of Dwayne, he returned to the mystery of Jerry. Kai and Theo solemnly led them to the back of the church, to a cemetery. Apollo found the stillness disturbing, especially among such obvious neglect. Layers of sunbaked leaves covered the graves, snapping like kettle-cooked chips as the crew traipsed forward. A loud rattle erupted from behind Apollo, sending him sprinting into Theo, who laughed.

"Did you guys not hear that?" Apollo asked, scanning the ground. "I think it might have been a rattlesnake."

Kai joined Theo in laughter. Zed chuckled, tapping Apollo on the shoulder with a spray paint canister. Apollo frowned, embarrassed. He should have recognized that noise. "You guys are going to vandalize a grave? That's... I don't know about that."

Zed grabbed his hand, leading him to a small headstone engraved, HERE LIES JERRY URICH. 2001–2017. Apollo stared at the grave, squeezing Zed's hand. He was stunned by how pristine the headstone was. It was made of iron, but it shone like alabaster. Even the leaves around the grave seemed immaculate, holy.

Zed was silent as paint sprayed from the canister, bathing the headstone in a coat of sanguine red. Apollo closed his eyes. A few feet away, Kai and Theo stood quietly. Apollo wondered if this was some sort of initiation. Were the Celestials a gang? He thought they just liked the name because they smoked a lot.

Was he about to be jumped? And how much paint was in that damn can? The sharp hiss was relentless, a sample looped for too long. Or was that just Kai and Theo continuing to laugh? He didn't know. His eyes were closed.

He opened them to find Zed standing completely still, her bony knees locked stiffly like the legs of a card table. "Come here," she grunted over her shoulder, contorting her torso and offering her hand. Apollo stepped forward uneasily, scrutinizing Zed's reddened palm.

"There's no way Jerry, whoever he was, deserved that," he stammered. "Seriously, guys, what the fuck is this? Two crimes in one day? Are we career criminals now?"

"Shut up, Apollo," Kai said, approaching the grave. "Your homepage is The Pirate Bay. That's crime. Graffiti is more like a public service."

"This is a private graveyard," Apollo retorted.

"Graffiti doesn't believe in privacy, dipshit. And neither did Jerry. He always said he wanted to be cremated and spread into a river, but his mom buried him because she got a discount from the church. So we bury her bullshit."

"Um, sure, but who the fuck is Jerry? You're talking like this nigga was Master Splinter."

"Jerry was who brought us all together," Theo interjected. "He and I used to take tennis lessons in East Point when I first moved here. He was from Riverdale, like you guys. He introduced me to Zed and Kai and Sol, and we all had the same private coach in Pointe South after our East Point coach retired. He was on the tennis team with them back at your school before you got skipped and Sol got locked up and he got…"

"Shot," Zed finished. "We were at AMC Southlake, heading to the car after seeing a movie, and he tried to break up a fight in the parking lot. It wasn't even some heroic shit. They were just by his car. Three white dudes, two-on-one. And a cop got there and just let loose, no warning. We heard the shots before we even saw him. Jerry died on the spot. We didn't even get to thank him for driving."

Apollo stood still, unsure whether to ask for more details or to offer hugs. He looked over at Kai and Theo. Their smiles were gone. They'd been hiding this pain from Apollo for two whole years. Did they not trust him? They did everything together, every day. He knew their Twitter passwords and their home security codes. Could there really be a greater level of intimacy? Apollo examined them further. Maybe they had been hiding the pain from themselves, too. Maybe they were protecting him. There had to be some explanation.

Zed approached him, removing another paint canister from her bag and offering it to him. He nodded and accepted the can. Walking toward the grave, he shook it vigorously, gripping it tightly despite his sweaty palms. Impatiently, he painted a single giant C, its blackness defiantly erupting from the headstone's fresh red coat. Apollo was angry—with his friends, with the situation, with how he knew the rest of the story would unfold.

Back in Zed's car, Apollo frowned as he scoured the web for more details on the shooting. It hadn't even been covered by the *Atlanta Journal-Constitution.* He found a brief blurb in the *Clayton News Daily,* the unwanted paper that his parents used to pay him to remove from the yard, his first chore. He didn't read it; the headline said enough. "Grand jury declines to indict Morrow cop."

Heated, he reached to adjust the temperature, mistakenly touching the radio dial instead. "Never touch a black woman's radio," Zed said in mockery of Kai, her unnatural neck roll selling the joke. Apollo moved his hand to her exposed thigh, giving it a gentle squeeze.

He quickly removed his hand as they pulled into Zed's driveway, where her mother and younger brother stood, eyeing them blankly. Apollo stared at the paint on his hands, unsure of what to do, especially once he realized he'd left a black handprint on Zed's thigh. Zed was already outside of the car. He joined her and her family, waving at her mother, Mrs. Pang, as her younger brother, Tim, voiced his disapproval.

"You went paintballing without me again? Ughhh."

"Sorry, kid, you've got to be at least seventeen."

"But Apollo just turned seventeen last October, and he's been going since last July!" Tim complained. Apollo stiffened, taking a quick glance at Mrs. Pang, who seemed to share Tim's skepticism. This paintball alibi was losing steam that it barely had to begin with.

"Apollo looks older though, Tim, so my friend who gives us the hookup can get away with letting Apollo through because he won't get carded again. Give it a break, kid. Three more years and you're in." She gave his forehead a slight nudge and stepped past him, toward the front door. Apollo followed, offering Tim a shrug. He was just glad no one had mentioned the handprint.

They immediately headed up the spiral staircase, proceeding past chronologically arranged family portraits and award certificates. Apollo always marveled at the strange sequence. In just fourteen steps, he would see Zed and Tim grow up and Mr. and Mrs. Pang's restaurant become more successful. His dad always made family seem like such a burden, but Zed's parents presented family as fundamental to success. Even the drunken cousin who Mr. Pang regularly scolded at barbecues was featured on the wall. Everybody got acknowledged.

Apollo walked past Zed's room and entered the bathroom, humming to himself as he dutifully scrubbed black paint from his large palms. He entered Zed's room to find her rifling through her dresser, looking back and forth between her phone and unfolded clothes.

"I can't believe I used to wear this shit," she said, shaking her head and holding up a fishnetted black blouse studded with dull spikes. "It looks like a level from *Twisted Metal*." She didn't even smile at the comparison, she was that disgusted. Apollo chuckled as she flung the shirt over her head. Her goth days were an endless source of self-shame—and humor.

"I wish Theo didn't send emails from his phone. It always cuts out the previous message for some reason. I think this is everything, though," Zed said, gesturing toward a pile on the ground. Apollo could barely discern individual articles of clothing. He just saw a mass of black. She really was committed to this grown woman shit. "Let's go to your house and get your stuff," Zed said.

Apollo winced. He knew that no one was home, but he was convinced that his mom could smell when he'd been around a girl. Even when he wore the sensory bludgeon known as AXE body spray, his mom could quickly parse through the overpowering fragrance and find a faint trace of lavender body wash or cherry lip gloss that had rubbed off on him. He didn't want to risk it.

His dad hadn't quite told him to get a new girlfriend when he saw his and Zed's prom pictures, but it was implied. "You need to be serious," he'd said. "Be serious" was a phrase that his dad tended to use whenever Apollo expressed interest in something that wasn't explicitly Nigerian. Apollo had never been given a definition, but he knew what it meant. Video games weren't serious. Building computers wasn't serious. Skateboarding wasn't serious—unless the X Games were on; his dad loved *other* people on skateboards. Cambodian girlfriends definitely weren't serious.

"Now's not a good time. My bathroom's dirty…"

"Okay," Zed said, interrupting him. "I'll meet you at Kai's house." She didn't press like she usually did, but he could tell she was upset. She'd get over it, though. She always did.

She embraced him and led him down the stairs, stopping on the second step from the bottom to kiss him at eye level, a feat that was impossible at their normal heights. "We're here for you, Apollo," she said as he stepped outside. Apollo turned and smiled, her family smiling back at him, their faces encased in the distant hope of 1997.

o o o

KAI ROSE SILENTLY, STEPPING CAREFULLY TO ALLOW Theo and Zed's naps to continue undisturbed. Even without the air conditioning on, Theo had immediately fallen asleep on the couch. And when Zed had come over, she quickly followed suit, staking out her own side of the sofa and curling up like a heated shrimp. Ever since graduation, they'd all been subject to these sudden fits of fatigue. Kai hadn't been tired this time, but she understood. From Jerry's death to Sol's imprisonment, they'd had an exhausting four years.

She opened the door and welcomed Apollo. He had also taken a nap; Kai could see the weariness tarrying on his face. And he had just woken up. His backpack was barely zipped.

"What are you kids up to tonight?" Mr. Forrester boomed from the back of the house as Kai and Apollo walked through the kitchen.

"Date night, Dad," Kai yelled back.

"What did I tell you about yelling?" Mr. Forrester said, his voice closer. "Shouting is to be louder, yelling is to be angrier." Stepping into the kitchen, he nodded at Apollo, cheesing. Kai didn't reciprocate.

"So, what's the date tonight? Dinner and a movie?"

"Actually, it's dinner and a movie and a movie," Kai told him. "There's a double feature down at Landmark downtown. *Total Recall* with Arnold and *Total Recall* with Colin."

"Yuck. And dinner?" Mr. Forrester asked.

"Undecided."

"Well, when you decide, text me. I might need you to bring me something back. Your mom was supposed to pick something up, but she had to run to your aunt's house. Who knows when she'll be back. Don't bring me back no Waffle House, though. I'm too old for that," he said, gesturing toward the bathroom.

Kai grimaced and walked to the living room, where she found Theo and Zed finally awake. She pointed at the clock, snapping them to attention. It was 7:38 p.m. "Later, Dad," she announced as they filed out the door. She made sure it was a shout.

A quick fifteen minutes later and they were at Sol's Waffle House again. Sol was waiting outside, no longer wearing her uniform, circling the parking lot on a bike. "We can't carry that," Theo quickly told her, rolling down his window as he and Kai pulled into the lot. Sol shrugged, returning it to its place near the front door. "It's stolen anyway," Kai heard her mutter.

Sol opened the back door on the passenger's side and slid in. "Nice," she said, fingering the bright red hairs of Kai's new wig. "I think we're ready." Theo nodded then calmly reversed, veering left onto Old National and then right onto the on-ramp for I-85 North.

Traffic was light. Theo hugged the passing lane for the entire trip, his speed undisturbed by slow drivers or lurking cops, a rare experience. Eventually, he got off on Stanton Road, heading north toward Campbellton. He hit a right on Campbellton then teetered onto Central Villa, a side street, slowing down and parking. Apollo and Zed pulled in front of him. Kai and Sol sat quietly as he turned off his GPS, turned on the GPS blocker Apollo had gotten from god-knows-where, and made a call using one of the burners. "I'm here," he said briefly. A gruff voice mumbled to him on the other end, then he hung up.

"Is everything good?" Sol asked, leaning over the armrest.

"Yeah," Theo said, looking into his side mirrors. Kai could tell he was nervous. He didn't know this area or this guy they were meeting; he probably couldn't even name a rapper from this part of the city. She damn sure couldn't. Sol leaned back, clearly unpersuaded. Kai didn't blame her.

A slate-colored Astro van coasted up behind them, creeping up to the bumper and flashing its lights. Kai watched the side mirror as Theo got out to meet the driver.

"George," she heard the driver say as his reflection stuck his hand out his window, the van's engine still grumbling.

"Jack," Theo replied, meeting George's hand with his own. They seemed to find comfort in their mutual deceptions.

"So, Jack, you got the money?" George asked.

"Yep, all I need are the keys," Theo responded.

"Good. I filled her up, got her some oil, and cleaned her out. Should be good to go."

"Okay," Theo said, brandishing his wallet. He removed ten one-hundred-dollar bills and counted them aloud, slowly. George silently watched. When Theo finished, George turned off the car and stepped out, handing him the keys. He was a strange man. Kai couldn't tell his age. But his wardrobe, a breezy linen suit with impeccably white Pumas and Adidas high socks, placed him somewhere between thirty-two and thirty-nine. *He probably has a Freaknik shirt,* she thought.

Theo took the keys and climbed into the van, testing the engine with a few revs. It sounded fine. Kai could sense his satisfaction. The air conditioning must have been on. Satisfied, he climbed down, putting the cash in George's hand. George quickly pocketed it, nodding his head. He started to walk off, but then he took out three hundred dollars and handed it back to Theo. "The brakes don't work so well," he said cryptically, again turning to walk away. He quickly disappeared around the block.

Theo hopped back into the van. Kai and Zed joined him, gas containers in tow, eager. Finally, it was going down.

"You gave Apollo your keys, right?" Theo asked, watching Zed fumble with the front passenger seat seat belt. She nodded affirmatively, clicking the buckle into place. Theo turned his eyes to the rearview mirror. "And Sol has my keys, right?"

He flinched as his question was answered by a hellish flash from his Civic's bright brake lights. "Yep!" Kai chortled. Theo cracked a smile, his nervousness dissolving.

Theo started the van, accelerating and turning into the street in order to pull up beside Sol. Kai thought he was going to stop, but they kept rolling.

∘ ∘ ∘

"Typical," Sol sighed as she watched the van continue rolling despite the red gleam of its brake lights. Impatiently, she pulled out the burner she'd been given and dialed Andromeda, one of the phone's only two programmed numbers. Zed answered, muttering something about brakes. Sol didn't laugh as the van's taillights crawled out of sight. She placed Zed on hold and dialed Titan, the phone's other programmed number. Apollo answered, bewildered. She shushed him and explained the situation, along with a change of plans, hanging up before he could respond. Clicking back over to Zed, she commandeered the mission.

"Hop out the van. Now. I think you got got. Don't forget the gas!" she barked, ending the call.

Moments later, she heard a loud crash. Unfazed, she sat patiently, waiting. Apollo came first, sliding into the passenger's seat. A few minutes later, Zed,

Theo, and Kai reappeared, ambling toward the car in a cloud of sweat and defeat. "It's a bust," Theo declared, approaching the driver's side.

"Get in," Sol ordered, gesturing toward the back seat. Theo hesitated.

"But you're in my seat," he complained.

"Just fucking get in, dude," Apollo ordered. "Change of plans."

Theo obliged. Zed and Kai followed suit.

"This is what we're doing," Sol announced. "We're going to take Theo's car, do the tag, torch the car, then file a police report saying the car was stolen at gunpoint when we got out the car at the Fort McPherson MARTA station, headed to the movies. This is better than me wasting my time going to actually pick up movie tickets while you guys fuck this up."

"What about Zed's car?" Kai pondered aloud. Zed perked up, concerned.

"We're going to leave it here," Sol said, starting the engine and turning the car back toward Campbellton. "This neighborhood is fine. It's just old people and their ratchet grandkids."

"That's not very reassuring," Zed said.

Within minutes, they were at the entrance to Fort McPherson, an old military base that was being redeveloped into a movie studio.

Sol jerked right, then reversed onto Kenilworth Drive, aligning the car with the gated entrance, one hundred yards away. She examined the intersection multiple times, her neck oscillating up and down the quiet street. Campbellton was clear. Venetian was clear. Sol turned off the music then revved the engine.

Sol leaned over the armrest, inches from Apollo's face. "There's not like a barrier on the other side of this gate, right? I read that bases in Iraq sometimes have trick entrances and shit like that. I'm blaming you if this goes wrong," she warned.

Apollo nodded. "Tyler Perry's studio has been using this entrance to shuttle in producers and actors who don't want to be associated with Tyler Perry before signing a contract. Just yesterday, Aaron McGruder was here. I have satellite images to confirm it." Satisfied, Sol evacuated his personal space then abruptly accelerated, thrusting them forward across Campbellton and into the gate.

Metal met metal, producing a booming clang. But the car kept going. Sol was booking it, immediately executing her improvised plan. She felt calm as she saw everyone else assume their roles: Kai pulled up a map on her phone, barking out terse directions; Apollo frantically keyed away on the encrypted laptop, summoning images of schematics and documents with maddeningly long lines of code; Zed stretched her legs across the armrest, tightening her shoelaces. Only Theo was idle. Sol wasn't surprised. They were doing this all for him, but he really wasn't necessary.

CHAPTER 3
JUNE 14
9:22 P.M.
83°F

THE BATTERED CIVIC SWERVED INTO THE PARKING lot of a tired two-story brick building. Sol stopped, keeping the car running. She looked away as Zed leaned forward and kissed Apollo's neck then opened the car and sprinted toward the building. "She's got twenty minutes," Theo declared. "Let's make it count." Sol winced at Theo in the rearview mirror then drove the car back to the main road, making a left. He thought he was in charge again. Nah.

More weary brick buildings greeted them as they drove toward the Comm Center, the Army's former satellite communications hub. Sol peered out the window excitedly. She had never been on a military base before. She marveled at how vulnerable it looked. She'd expected turrets and glass shards and land mines, but this place looked like a college campus.

"Left," Kai quickly said.

"This fucking server better be here, Apollo," Sol growled as they approached the Comm Center.

o o o

APOLLO PAID SOL NO MIND. IN FIVE MINUTES, HE'D successfully jammed the base's ragtag video surveillance network, but he wanted to keep an eye on traffic. He knew that even if they weren't caught in the act, which was actually starting to seem possible, they also didn't need to be caught after the act. A cramped MINI Cooper wasn't exactly an ideal getaway car.

Sol stopped the car in front of a sleek modern building. The engine grumbled off. Apollo hopped out, his open laptop swinging unsteadily in his hands as he raced toward the entrance. Even though he knew he'd be able to hack the satellite as planned, he had to hack it while it was passing over Austell, Georgia, giving him a twenty-minute window. The problem was that he had no idea where the control server for the satellite was located within the building. WikiLeaks was always very forthcoming when it came to secret government programs and secret roads and secret plots, but secret building interiors were still beyond its means. Apollo exhaled heavily as he approached the door, passing a flagpole. The run had been farther than he thought. He wasn't sure if it was defensive design or the military just being extra. He decided to look it up later.

The door was unlocked. Apollo stepped into a bare lobby, furnished with a plain marble desk, folded plastic chairs, and a portrait of former president Barack Obama. "Damn, this place is old," Apollo muttered.

The only indicator that this building had previously been occupied by the military was its presence on the base. It easily could have been a generic office building. Apollo feared the worst. The military had cleaned this place out, he knew it. He anxiously ran toward the elevators, pressing the call button and searching for a directory. He sweated profusely; the AC was very off. The building had ten floors, but the directory was blank, erased. Lone letters lingered like unfinished alphabet soup, but they were too scattered to be decoded. Apollo mashed the call button.

The elevator arrived, and he stepped in, eyeing the access panel then checking the time. He had fifteen minutes to find the server, hijack the satellite, and tag Six Flags as planned. It wasn't enough. He stopped to focus. Webpages, codes, and images of Zed flashed in his head. His heart was beating so fast he could feel his pulse in his right eye. After three silent minutes, he pressed the button for the second floor, reasoning that the floor with the servers would be excessively air-conditioned. The second-floor doors opened. Apollo felt no change in temperature, so he pressed the button for the third floor. Again, no change. He had seven floors and twelve minutes left. He began to feel his pulse in both eyes.

The eighth floor greeted him with a blast of chilled air. He ran into a dimly lit hallway, his worn gray Vans skidding as he abruptly halted in front of the only door in sight. Apollo sighed as the ice-cold doorknob obligingly turned. He'd found it.

Tall black servers lined the room like library bookshelves, haughtily stretching toward the ceiling. After plugging in his laptop, Apollo quickly leaped over the firewall, connecting to the local network and accessing the satellite. He had nine minutes. His fingers pecked at the keyboard, summoning the satellite's celestial eye. Faint lights and dark green shapes scurried across his retina as he initiated the satellite's onboard laser. Apollo stopped to take it all in.

How could Atlanta be so large, yet so small in his mind? Activating the laser, he gasped, shocked that it was real, quickly laughing at the absurdity of his surprise. The government had an actual weaponized laser in space, and he was not only controlling it, he was about to do graffiti with it. Even after all this planning and research, it was still jarring.

The burner rang, directing Apollo's attention to the time. "Fuck!" he screamed, ignoring the call. He'd blown it. The satellite was now too far east to accurately hit their chosen target; the margin of error was too high outside of the measured time window. He'd triple-checked. He violently kicked one of the servers, then stared at the phone, an ancient Nokia with a sickly green glow that dully radiated from its plain screen. The missed call was from Andromeda, the phone that had been assigned to Zed. He couldn't call her back. Tasked with manually shutting down the satellite's remote access panel and then running two and a half miles to the Comm Center, she had been the most at risk. She could have taken a fist or a Taser or a golf cart or a bullet. Apollo would not let her down.

Pocketing his phone, he sat down, his eyes lingering on the satellite's continuing images of Atlanta.

Running trails and camping grounds trickled into his view. He knew this place. It was Stone Mountain Park, the site of his first mosquito bite and premier destination for the occasional white power rally.

He acted quickly, directing the satellite's eye to the park's main attraction: the mountain. Entering the coordinates, he activated the laser, impatiently waiting for it to finalize. Scripts scurried across his screen like excited ants then abruptly stopped, replaced by a static blackness. Apollo gawked at the screen, disappointed. There hadn't even been an *Are you sure you want to do this?* message. The government continued to disappoint him.

A magnificent orange pillar suddenly erupted into view, ripping through the firmament and descending onto the park with unnatural fury, plowing into the mountain. Even from his proxy celestial perch, Apollo could feel the destruction being wrought, the stone and sediment becoming mobile after millennia of stasis. An entire ecosystem of birds seemed to retreat into the sky, fleeing the devastation. Apollo watched in awe as the air along the beam's path quivered, it too touched by the beam's furious omnipotence. He swore to never again shake an aerosol can. He had felt subversive before, but this was power. He was no longer marking territory; he was seizing it from the earth, altering it in his image.

Apollo was entranced by the laser's raw power. Time unwound as he watched the geyser of light glide across the earth, his screen shaking as the beam pulverized the mountain and its surroundings. The feed lacked audio, but that put Apollo at ease; the drone bombings he'd seen were also soundless. After three sublime minutes, the pillar of light dissolved to black, and a smile crawled from Apollo's eyes to his lips as he saw a distinct shape take form.

o o o

"He fucked up. Let's leave him," Sol suggested.

"Fuck you," Zed huffed, her utter seriousness obvious despite her heaving breaths. Theo squeezed Kai's hand. Everything was going downhill. Sol was acting crazy, Zed said the remote access panel had been removed, and Apollo wasn't answering his phone. He felt trapped. They had to get off this base before it got worse.

Kai spoke up, her voice confident. "Apollo's fine. Traffic looks normal around Six Flags, but Stone Mountain is looking wild. I think Apollo might have upgraded their weird laser show." She passed her phone to Sol, who stared blankly at the sea of red dots forming around the mountain's winding roads.

"Not bad," Sol admitted. "Let's just hope he was smart enough to leave Z, E, and D out of his tag." They laughed.

Tension returned as they heard the frantic thump of shoes hitting concrete. Apollo was sprinting toward the car at top speed, spittle leaking from his mouth alongside garbled words. "Drive!" he demanded when he reached the vehicle, slamming his hand on the car's roof and jumping into the passenger's seat. Sol reacted quickly, starting the car and veering out of the parking lot in one cool motion.

"What happened?" Theo asked.

"Tyler Perry bought the rights to *The Boondocks*."

Zed swung at the back of Apollo's neck with an open palm, the smack resonating with the dull sound of flesh hitting flesh. Apollo didn't say anything, but Theo swore he could still hear echoes from the slap.

Sol smashed the throttle as they headed back toward their entrance, then slowed to a crawl as they neared the gate. The gate was still mangled, but Campbellton was clear. There were neither cops in the bushes nor concerned citizens on the sidewalk. As expected, this part of the city didn't produce patriots. Theo wasn't surprised; it didn't even produce rappers.

To Theo, their arrival at Zed's car seemed instantaneous. He asked Sol to allow him one final ride. She agreed, leaving the keys in the ignition and stepping out to join Zed and Apollo, who were walking toward Zed's car. Kai remained in the back seat.

Theo got out the car and stretched. A slight breeze grazed his face, momentarily cooling the hot night. It wasn't enough. A thin layer of sweat insisted on forming. He sighed. The entire ordeal had taken a little over a half hour, but Theo felt like he had aged a year. He leaned on the roof of the car, taking it all in. Both his graduation money and now his car were gone. Maybe even his life, if this night had any more surprises. This wasn't even remotely how his summer before college was supposed to go. At least he had those three C-notes?

Kai tapped on the back window, gesturing for him to get back into the car. They needed to leave. Theo slid into the driver's seat, flustered. Did they really have to destroy the car? A nigga in a busted Civic was as natural as algae in a creek. What wasn't natural was going to the police station to report a fake crime on the same night you committed a real crime. Wasn't there a Biggie song about that? And Apollo had disabled the base's surveillance, hadn't he? They had gotten away with it, definitely. Probably. If they hadn't, that laser would have already gotten them, probably before they even got off the base. Excessive precaution could be just as dangerous as naivete. Theo made up his mind. No need to get all surgical with it, throwing body parts to unfed pigs. The night was a success. Theo cranked the engine and pulled out slowly.

"Where are we going?" Kai asked. Theo stared straight ahead. For once, he knew where he was headed.

The wrecked van was just as they'd left it, implanted in the trunk of a tree at the bottom of the hill on Central Villa. Theo slowed and parked on the side of the road. Kai removed her flaming red wig and shook out her curls. They exited the car, reaching the trunk in two exhausting steps. Goddamn, it was hot.

Gasoline containers in tow, they quickly emptied them on the wreckage as Zed, Apollo, and Sol watched from inside the MINI. Theo watched Kai place her gas container on the ground then walk over to Zed's car, sticking out her hand. The driver's window slid down and her hand was quickly filled with two phones and a laptop. "That's not all the gas, right?" Theo heard Sol ask. Kai ignored her and sprinted to the van, emptying her hands. The electronics hit the ground with a dull, unsatisfying thud. She gave her burner, the only one that was a smartphone, a particularly strong toss. It had come preloaded with MapQuest; it deserved the worst. Theo smiled when the screen shattered on impact.

Retrieving her gas container, Kai used the last few drops to douse the wig. Brandishing her lighter, she lit it then tossed it into the wreckage.

She and Theo swiftly filed back into his car. Following Kai's directions, he pulled out quickly and headed toward Cascade Road. Theo hoped for an explosion, but he had watched enough *Mythbusters* to know better. Instead, he listened as Kai watched videos of their laser tag on Twitter. He couldn't wait to see what the tag said in the morning, and he couldn't wait to see Sol's response to the change of the change of plans. He hated when she stepped up to solve his problems.

I-285 appeared quickly, and the seven miles home seemed to appear even quicker, but even as the night glided by, Theo remained in that harrowing half hour. When his head finally hit his pillow after dropping off Kai and driving to Marietta, he didn't feel relaxed. He felt poised, ready to take on whatever else the summer dared to offer and determined not to fuck it up.

CHAPTER 4
JUNE 15
12:59 A.M.
77°F

The headache was instantaneous. She had no voicemails, but Tilly Erickson knew that nineteen missed calls from Rick at 1 a.m. couldn't be anything other than trouble. Scrabbling through her nightstand, she found some loose pills and tossed them back, hoping they were Advils and not the leftover ibuprofens from her root canal. She didn't check.

Her temple continued to thump as she made her way downstairs, heading to her work desk. She had left DC so she could avoid nights like this, but Atlanta was rarely the dream destination people wanted it to be, even for FBI agents.

Easing into her office chair, she turned on her computer and logged into the FBI remote server, opening other tabs to catch up on news while she waited for access to her inbox. Three-step authentication was great for security, but awful for end users.

"Atlanta is nothing but traffic and fraud, my ass," she muttered aloud, shutting her laptop. She didn't even need to log in to the server. The news had told her enough. Leaving her phone on her desk, she headed back to bed. This might be her last opportunity for sleep.

By 6 a.m., the missed call count had expanded to twenty-four. Tilly moved quickly, darting between the bedroom and the bathroom, gathering clothes and cosmetics.

At 6:22 a.m., she was in her car, a Cadillac STS, racing toward the office. Buford Highway was chillingly empty. For four miles, Tilly didn't see a single car in the parking lots of its endless shopping plazas. And the only vehicles on the road itself were MARTA buses, which seemed to rejoice in the ambient desertion, zooming past vacant bus stops at breakneck speeds. The number of cars slightly increased as she turned onto Clairmont Road, but Tilly still felt unsettled. She'd always wished for a better commute, but this was damn near teleportation.

Century Parkway appeared quickly. Tilly parked and entered her office building, laughing at herself for wearing heels on a day when there was no one present to impress or command.

Rick was sitting in her office, in the sole guest chair, wearing running shorts, a polo, and worn sneakers, along with a shoulder holster. Tilly went to her desk without greeting him.

"Why does your voicemail say 'Call me back!' if you know you're not going to answer?"

"Because I don't believe coworkers should text."

Rick sucked his teeth. "You're a real piece of work, Erickson. I guess I'll fax you the status report then. Since you only read emails from your phone, I might instigate an ethical crisis if I email it to you. Technically, sending government emails to your phone isn't allowed since our emails are government property, but hackers get to do what they want, right?"

Tilly didn't respond. She'd never arrived at the office this early. Her ritual of applying her makeup using her unlit monitor didn't quite work without a surfeit of morning light. It was only 6:43 a.m. Her eyebrows would have to wait at least another hour. Ready to tolerate Rick, she turned to face him, his eyes already on her.

"What do we know?" she asked him.

As usual, his answer was long.

"Not much. A weaponized government satellite was hacked from Fort McPherson and used to make some sort of giant J on Stone Mountain. The Confederate memorial on the mountain was damaged in the process. Even the horses got scorched. There's a torched van in South Atlanta near the fort. Real South Atlanta, near East Point, not fucking Henry County, by the way. Some phones and a laptop were found, but they won't be telling us much, if you know what I mean. They were toasty! There's no footage of the culprits. McPherson's whole cybersecurity network was pretty much defanged because of the movie studio work being done there, so it was easily jammed. Apparently, no one learned anything from the Sony hack. There are some car parts near where the culprits broke the fort's barricade for their entrance, but there's more cars in this city than people, so that's probably a dead end. Local cell towers don't paint much of a picture either. When cell towers started going up around there, the military had them equipped with scrambling devices so no communications could be intercepted. So that's basically the best place in the city to commit a crime. Other than like, I don't know, Old National? I'll check the stats later. I'd personally argue that Buckhead is the best place. It has the city's highest concentration of single white women. No one believes me because I'm a black man and, clearly, I have a personal interest in passing the torch, but I swear on my life that single white women are this country's next criminal class. Their crimes may look personal and passionate on Lifetime, but out here in the real world, white girls be scheming. You saw *Spring Breakers*, right? I didn't, but I think I know what it was about, you know? I heard Gucci did well…"

He continued. "The airport is still open, surprisingly. But people aren't flying, no surprise. Giant death beams from the sky are a lot harder to ignore than high prices and a big ass terminal. We're not technically under a state of emergency, but even Waffle Houses are closed, so do technicalities even really apply? Um, that's about it. Oh, and this is our case. Like you and me. NSA thought about picking up, then the Pentagon, then Quantico, but it looks pretty clusterfucked, so it got rolled down to us. They've been trying to close this office for a while anyway. About damn time. We've got a press conference at nine. I'm glad you wore heels. You don't see a lot of tall black women on TV these days. That's it!"

"Okay," Tilly replied, gesturing toward the doorway. Rick Herrington was only tolerable in small doses. Rick sauntered out, leaving Tilly in silence. It was only 6:46. Goddamn, he talked fast. Tilly reached across her desk and grabbed her name plaque, fixating on the engraved words: "Tilly Erickson, Senior Agent, Cybercrimes Division." She'd finally gotten a case worth her rank, but it had all this damn baggage.

o o o

Zed watched the press conference for #FireAndBrimStoneMountain, as it was now being called, from her computer. Apollo had told them they couldn't ever discuss the past night via an electronic device, but that didn't mean she couldn't read about it. At the podium stood a freckled woman with exquisite eyebrows. She insisted that there wasn't a story to follow. Zed chuckled as she dryly answered questions from the press, even the silly ones.

"Was this a terrorist attack?" a reporter asked.

"Perhaps," the woman said.

"Is Atlanta safe?"

"Hopefully."

"Was this an extraterrestrial event?"

"Absolutely."

"As in aliens?"

"No."

"Do you know what extraterrestrial means?"

"Yes."

"Are Southern values under attack?"

"Cheap gas is the only Southern value."

"Does the Stone Mountain incident have any relation to the fire off of Campbellton Road?"

The woman paused. "I am not aware of the fire to which you refer," she belted out, robotically.

"Fuck, they already have leads," Zed shrieked, slamming her laptop shut. This was the last thing she needed on a day she'd have to spend at home with her parents. They always knew when something was troubling her, and once they knew, they found out. Frantically, Zed paced around her room, seeking some sort of escape from her thoughts and her house. She decided to go see Apollo. Today would be the day she met his parents. She didn't care whether he liked it or not.

Getting dressed was easier than she expected. She settled on flip-flops and a simple black smock, cute but not flashy. Her hair was trickier. Buns, her go-to hairdo, made her feel confident, but she didn't want his parents to think she was controlling. His dad always sounded somewhat scared of assertive women. But he also sounded like an asshole. He could probably use a scare. Zed decided to go with buns. On her way out, she exchanged her flip-flops for her black combat boots. Confidence required an ensemble.

The walk to his house was refreshing. Driveways were empty and people were outside, unfazed by the events of the previous night. Zed was pleased. The empty lanes and parking lots being looped on

Twitter were unsettling. Graffiti wasn't supposed to scare people. It was supposed to show them that nothing was permanent, that small acts could alter the world. Zed didn't know if the neighborhood *really* got it—after all, unlike her parents and Apollo's parents, who were dentists, some people just couldn't afford to miss work—but at least she knew she didn't live in a neighborhood full of pussies.

Apollo's dad answered the door. He was a squat man; his limbs hung close to his torso as if they were scared to grow further. "What?" he asked Zed.

"Hello, sir, I am Zadie. I'm here to see Apollo," she answered politely.

"Cindy, Apollo's playmate is here. Please deal with her," he commanded, turning around and leaving the door ajar. Zed stepped into the foyer, her boots loudly echoing on the marble floor. The house had the same design as hers, but something felt off. The stairs seemed steeper, the windows seemed sealed shut. The walls were coated in a metallic black, making all instances of color look like tiny supernovae. Zed frowned at the image of her black smock in the mirror.

"Shoes, please," Apollo's mother said, entering the foyer and pointing at a half-full shoe rack to the left of the front door. "I'm Cindy," she continued, offering her hand after nudging the door closed. She wore a brilliant pink maxi dress with two lavender stripes running down the sides and lavish black heels. Zed was both impressed and ashamed on sight.

Zed shook Cindy's hand firmly, meeting her intense eyes directly. She was a tall woman, bony yet imposing. She was so tall that her head seemed to float above her body, connected by will rather than sinew. Zed stammered out some small talk. "Did you hear about what happened in Stone Mountain?"

"Young lady, please remove your shoes." Zed immediately obliged, unlacing her boots and placing them on the shoe rack next to a rainbow of differently colored heels and worn brown sandals. Without her boots, she lost two inches of height, placing her farther beneath Cindy's formidable gaze. Cindy silently started up the stairs. Zed took the hint, trailing her.

There were no pictures on the stairwell, just blank space. Cindy stopped at a bedroom with a crimson door, silent.

"Hey Mom, what's up?" Apollo bellowed from the other side of the door.

"Your girlfriend is here. She dresses strangely."

Apollo careened out of the door, grabbing Zed like she was a freed hostage being released to the police, and slammed the door behind him. "Really?" he asked, burying his chin into her neck as he embraced her for a hug.

"I'd ask how'd it go, but they let you in the house, so that's a pretty good sign," he said, releasing her to step back and look her in the eyes. "*I* like your dress, by the way," he added. Zed shook her head and slid to the floor, sitting cross-legged, a flap of her smock splayed over her crotch. She scanned Apollo's room. It looked pretty bare for a place where he spent so much time. A mounted TV was the only wall ornament, and a bed, a desk, and a small dresser were the only furniture.

On the desk were three monitors, all of them powered on, and a PS4 on standby. Zed searched for some lone analog device, a clock or a tome of Apollo's beloved manga, finding nothing but more wires, screens, and devices. Theo wasn't joking. Apollo truly did live his life online. Zed faintly smiled as pictures of her and Apollo appeared on all of his screensavers.

"Are you okay?" Apollo asked. Zed wasn't sure how long he'd been staring at her.

"Yeah, I'm worried," she finally replied.

"You must have watched the press conference. I caught that too. Of course they have leads. We don't know if they're good leads, though."

"Yeah, I guess that's true," Zed said, unassured. "I'm just worried about the J. We might be in some Clayton County graffiti database or something. I know you put a C on it, but I feel like we should clear Jerry's grave, just to be safe."

Apollo cracked a smile. "Clayton County doesn't track graffiti. I've checked. ClayPo doesn't even have Windows 7 yet. And no one thinks of what we did as graffiti other than us and maybe some intern at *Jacobin*. So even if Jerry's mom turns us in, which she won't because we put a dead black boy on a racist mountain, what would she tell them? 'My son's old friends sprayed a giant C on his grave.' I think we're covered. Instead of sweating that, how about we look at some of these goofy-ass hashtags?"

Zed still felt uneasy, but looking at hashtags sounded fun. She scooted over as Apollo grabbed an iPad from under his pillow and queued up Twitter, joining her on the floor. Most of the jokes were forgettable, as ephemeral as the weak laughs they drew, but Zed enjoyed scrolling through them, watching people make sense of the world by making fun of it. #FireandBrimStoneMountain was the top trending topic, but the real jokes were at #IHadaBeam, which featured endless images of Dr. Martin Luther King Jr. spewing lasers upon national monuments. It was wack that humor was people's default reaction, Zed felt, but she understood its appeal. Laughter was like that brief moment of silence when you drove under a bridge during rain; it placed you outside of time even as it sped you through it.

Apollo gravitated toward the conspiracy tweets, the ones with ideas too nebulous to coagulate into hashtags. "The aliens are here bro. Future and Ciara were the first sign. I swear," tweeted one user. "2013: no braves. 2014: snowstorm. 2015: floods. 2016: Donald Glover is cool. 2017: falcons lose and bridge collapses. 2018: Childish Gambino making trap now, da fuck?. Stay woke," read another tweet. Apollo really got a kick out of that one, sprawling out on his floor as the laughter dispersed across his body. Zed snapped a photograph of him with her phone, studying it afterward. It was a keeper.

"Honestly, this isn't making me feel better," she confessed, standing up, her dress sliding back down to her ankles. Apollo flashed her a look from the floor, his eyebrows hoisted by concern. "I shouldn't have even come," she continued, stepping toward the door. Silent, Apollo remained on the carpet as she quickly left the room, closing the door. Her footsteps were muted as she slogged down the stairs in socks, but the eventual tap of her boots on the foyer was clear, undulating throughout the still house before terminating with a thud from the front door. On her way home, she examined her new photo. Softly illuminated by the dull flicker of his screens, Apollo looked blissful. Pocketing her phone, Zed wished she could say the same for herself.

CHAPTER 5
JUNE 15
10:03 A.M.
82°F

SOL TENSED IN RESPONSE TO THE CREAKING PORCH. She didn't recognize those footsteps. Bounding across her living room in three inaudible strides, she entered the kitchen and armed herself with a knife. The sharp scent of the onions she'd cut for breakfast lingered on its blade. The footsteps halted a few feet from the door, their echo drowning in the drone of the cicadas outside. Sol dropped to an alert crouch, the knife gripped tightly in her left hand. The unknown visitor exhaled deeply. It was a man. Sol remained in place, waiting for his next move.

A sharp jangle rang out. Keys. "Is he from the bank?" Sol mouthed to herself. Her dead grandmother continued to receive bank notices, but Sol never opened mail that wasn't hers. Her first cellmate, Laura, had gotten four years for that. The stranger casually unlocked the screen door. He hadn't even had to search for the right key; he already knew which one it was. Sol remained crouching, wondering who the hell was at her door.

Couldn't be cops. Except for last night and a few tags here and there—oh, and that bike—she'd been on her best behavior. Couldn't be Jehovah's Witnesses. They avoided that midday Georgia sun like it was a secular holiday. Couldn't be Antonio either. She'd always had him drop her off a few houses away. She'd dated him despite his rep, but she dumped him precisely because his rep turned out to be true. Who the fuck was at her door?

Loudly fiddling around, the stranger seemed to be unable to find the right key. Sol fumed. She wasn't about to go out like Copperhead, pounced on and then killed in her own damn home. Brazenly, she stood up and flung open the front door.

She was greeted by a shriek. Her older cousin, Derrick, stood on the other side of the storm door, bewildered. He'd gained weight, lots of it. He'd also acquired some money. Despite the heat, he was wearing a full suit, tailored and slick. He was still a chump, though. Sol laughed and invited him in. He tarried in the doorway.

"I thought you were in jail," Derrick said cautiously. Sol could feel his eyes on her chiseled arms.

"I was. Been back home for over a year, though. I just graduated. Three point four."

"A year? Shit. I had no idea."

"Really? Your dad picked me up."

"Weird. He never mentioned it."

Sol didn't respond. Stepping back, she invited Derrick in again. This time, he obliged, following her into the kitchen, where she deposited her knife onto a counter and reached inside the fridge, removing a jug of sweet tea. Raising the jug above her head, she offered Derrick a swig. He declined. Sol's sweet tea was notoriously more tea than sweet.

"So, why are you here, Derrick?" Sol asked, drinking straight from the jug. She neither offered Derrick a seat nor sat down herself.

"You remember my homeboy Mario? He said he had drove by here and Nana's house was all fixed up and shit. I knew your parents were thinking about fixing this place up, so I was curious about what it looked like."

"You see my parents lately?"

"Yeah, every couple of weeks or so. They're doing fine. You don't talk to them?"

Sol didn't respond, but her eyes remained on Derrick as if she were still speaking. He avoided her gaze, scanning the room. She watched as his eyes lingered on all of her renovations: new cabinets, new sink, new blender. She had seen that look before.

"So, how are your friends? What did you guys used to call yourselves? The Starjammers?"

Sol snorted out a laugh. "Nah, the Celestials."

"Because y'all all used to get mad high, right?"

"Sometimes. But the real story is that we all met playing tennis, and when we started out, we used to always hit the balls extra high. Like into the cosmos and shit."

"That's funny."

"I guess. They're fine. I saw them all last night. Good times."

"That's good. Family is here for you too, you know."

"That's good to know. I'll be sure to call you guys up the next time I'm going over best practices for stopping a home invasion or renovating a house on minimum wage. Get the fuck out of my house."

Derrick held his ground. "This ain't your house, Solara," he blurted out, emphasizing her name. Sol's eyes instinctively flitted to the knife on the counter, but her hands reached toward a drawer. Derrick flinched, his fleshy face jiggling from the suddenness of his movement.

Nana had bought a gun after Kathryn Johnston, an elderly woman, got killed by some trigger-happy Atlanta cops. And she used to keep it in this exact drawer. "Waiting on an order of pig ears," she always joked whenever someone inevitably stumbled upon it at a cookout. Sol knew Derrick had no idea the gun now resided under her pillow, so she let her hand linger in the drawer. He was such a pussy.

"Found it," she said excitedly, brandishing a wrinkled sheet of paper. She balled it up and tossed it at Derrick, who caught it with his forehead. Picking it up from the floor, he flattened it out, scanning its legalese.

Sol didn't feel like waiting. "That's a copy of the deed to the house. My house. Nana left this house to whoever in the family took care of it. All anyone had to do was stay here for forty-five days and show the bank that they were taking care of it." Derrick stared back at her quizzically. "I'm an eighteen-year-old homeowner, nigga," Sol added.

Derrick scoffed. "Good for you. I'm a twenty-eight-year-old with multiple homes. Call me when you get a degree or something," Derrick said coldly, crumpling then dropping the deed. He left just as quickly, his footsteps creaking more loudly than when he came. Sol slammed the door behind him and went to the window to watch his departure.

He'd been a pile of putty in her presence, but back in the outside world, his gait was confident, his arms and legs swinging freely like cooked noodles hanging from a fork. Sol seethed as she watched him start his car, a gleaming hybrid Hyundai Sonata, and back out into the street, probably headed to one of his many homes. Suddenly the two years she planned to wait before starting college seemed like an eternity. Even after an early release from juvie and an unlikely on-time graduation, she was still a failure. On edge, she walked to her grandmother's liquor cabinet and removed a small bottle of Jack Daniel's. The crumpled deed remained on the floor.

o o o

SOL HEARD FAMILIAR VOICES. "I WISH SHE WOULD hurry up," Kai complained. "These mosquitoes are killing me. Are you sure Waffle House is closed?"

"Yeah, it was on the news. I saw it when I was at Apollo's house."

Kai rang the doorbell, holding it down to extend the tinny chime. Sol finally rose from the couch. "Come in," she grumbled, opening the door. Zed and Kai entered the house, making a beeline to the couch. Sol remained standing, sluggish from her whiskey-induced nap. She glanced at the clock above the television. 4:24 p.m. She'd slept for six hours. Kai and Zed were in high spirits. To Sol, they seemed to glow.

"What's up with y'all today?" Sol asked, noticing they were both dressed in form-flattering nylon fitness gear and sneakers.

"Apollo…" Zed started.

"Tennis, my nigga," Kai interrupted.

Sol immediately shook her head. "I haven't played since, like, tenth grade, before I got locked up. You guys will murk me."

"Whatever, girl," Zed chided. "With those arms, you'll probably be acing us left and right. Remember the first time Theo got an ace? He lost the match, but he insisted that we go to Chick-fil-A to celebrate."

"Yeah, I remember that," Kai sighed. "I was the one who got aced by him! And hell yeah, he lost. I killed his ass. But y'all never remember my version. To this day, I'm convinced that the secret ingredient in that Chick-fil-A sauce is loyalty." Zed slid off the couch and dropped to her knees, propped up by the laughter bouncing around her chest.

Sol quietly belched, shaking her head again. The tennis talk and the Jack were bringing up memories of Jerry. "Tennis Titan," she'd used to call him. He actually wasn't particularly good at the sport. As Sol improved her game, she realized that Jerry's only skill was his reaction time. He didn't control space like a veteran player. He simply defended it well, chasing the ball to every crevice and cranny of the court like a determined puppy. His pursuit of the ball was so dogged that he seemed to forget the possibility of injury. Matches with him used to last forever because even if he was obviously outmatched, he'd trap his opponent in a purgatory of deuce, refusing to relinquish a game until his opponent collapsed from fatigue or frustration.

His specialty was the high-flying return lob. No matter how impossible the odds were of him reciprocating a well-placed shot, he'd accelerate toward it at inhuman speed, committing life, limb, and racket to a cloud-chafing return that would make the ball linger in the air like an escaped balloon, then casually glide back toward the court like a Tony Parker teardrop. His opponent would then smash it when it finally touched down and repeat the cycle. Their coach used to call it the float-a-dope method, much to Jerry's goofy satisfaction.

"I just can't, guys. I'll go and watch you," Sol offered, slipping on some worn flats.

"That works!" Kai said, leaping from the couch and heading toward the door. Her head suggestively turned from the open liquor cabinet to Sol, but she didn't say anything. Sol didn't either.

Zed followed behind Kai, twirling her car keys. Sol stayed behind to take a quick swig. Her empty stomach erupted into a ruckus as the whiskey slithered down her throat, but she felt calm. Derrick could wait.

o o o

Zed drove cautiously, the FBI press conference from earlier still haunting her. It was midafternoon, but traffic was light. Maybe Riverdale was more spooked than she realized. *All Things Considered*, her favorite NPR show, took on a new meaning as she noticed the traffic cameras at every stop along Highway 85. She'd never been pulled over before, but the ambient gaze of the law suddenly seemed to be confronting her head-on, vis-à-vis.

Her anxiety brought back memories of the day in fourth grade when she realized that her classmates knew she was Asian. She thought she had camouflaged herself well, hiding in plain sight among the Mexicans and Puerto Ricans, but when she took out some khmer num krok at lunch, the eyes that fell on her were observational, not incidental. They were still friendly eyes, but she could sense the re-sorting, the recategorization. Nothing was the same. Within days, the boys were suddenly eager to discuss anime and video games, and the girls wanted to talk about K-pop and skincare.

Zed had survived and eventually thrived in this odd environment, but not without effort. In order to thwart the egg roll jokes and the dumb questions about the geometric orientation of her vagina, she'd had to learn how to see herself as she was seen. It wasn't too hard, especially since most people weren't particularly committed to how they initially saw her, but Zed had always wanted to reverse the situation, to wield that power of seeing rather than just redirecting it in her favor. Last night, Apollo had briefly wielded it. She'd have to ask him about it, maybe experience it herself.

Highway 279 slowly eased into sight. Zed hit a right and continued toward Kenwood Park, their destination. She hated that she had to go all the way to another county for a decent park, but Kai refused to play at Flat Shoals, and Sol was banned from Independence Park for life.

The park was active. The sun had reached its merciful phase, its rays suddenly inviting after a day-long barrage of heat. Zed, Sol, and Kai filed out of the MINI armed with rackets, water bottles, and tennis balls. Noticing that the tennis courts were momentarily empty, Zed gestured for Sol and Kai to pick up the pace. Unwanted whistles and stares grazed them as they passed the fenced basketball court. "This is for you, Charlie's Angels!" a shirtless white guy shouted at them, launching a three-point shot. It air-balled spectacularly, slinking toward the ground like a Raid-rinsed wasp. The other players laughed, but their stares intensified as the girls' backsides came into view. Zed could feel their eyes on her ass. Sol rolled her shoulders back and hurled her arms skyward, extending her middle fingers.

"Fuck Fayette County," Zed huffed, walking onto the tennis court.

"Word. It's just Clayton County with golf carts," Kai seconded. "And nice tennis courts."

o o o

THE TENNIS COURT WAS THOROUGHLY BAKED. SOL slumped to the hot ground, convinced her ass would catch on fire. Her mind started to swelter as well. What had Derrick been doing? Sol concentrated on Kai and Zed's forms, hoping they could keep her from feeling violent.

Kai's strokes were works of art, kinetic compositions. The fabric of reality seemed to dissolve and reform when she hit the ball, redirecting Zed's wild shots with an impossible calmness. Sol remembered Zed as a staunch fundamentalist. Her frantic shots were a new development. Even if the ball's trajectory was obvious, she would decide how to hit it at the last second. It was an odd style, but Sol could see its utility. Kai was returning the shots every time, but each return was less strategic and more reactive. Sol couldn't believe these were just warm-up shots. She'd missed so much while she was away.

"First to eight games, win by two, switch every odd game," Zed announced.

"Yep," Kai agreed, throwing her racket into the air. "W."

The racket clattered onto the ground, the "W" of the Wilson emblem facing down. She'd lost the toss. "Your serve," Zed decided. Solemnly, they lined up on opposite ends of the court, tapping their rackets on the ground in tandem, their ritual.

"Love, love!" Kai roared, tossing the ball into the air and pummeling it toward the earth. It landed directly in front of Zed, who sidestepped it and responded with a quick backhand.

Sol's neck stiffened as she watched the ball continually whizz over the net, propelled by grunts and devastating swings. Zed and Kai were only on the first point, but they were playing as if the point decided the match.

"Hey, Angel," someone whispered to Sol. She turned around, fists clenched. The white guy from the basketball court smiled back at her through the fence, his eyes scanning her body, the sweat on his unformed muscles gleaming in the dim sunlight. Sol stood, meeting his gaze. He was shorter than she was.

"You girls from around here?" he stammered, feigning coolness. His eyes plunged to his feet like anchors in air as Sol silently stared him down, her arms crossed.

He spoke rapidly, his words dropping from his mouth like loose change from an overturned purse. "I'm throwing a party tonight. It will be pretty casual. Lots of guys. Only ten bucks."

Sol remained silent, her gaze unbroken. "Lots of girls too…" he added.

The silence continued. "We're not paying to get into a rando house party," Sol finally said.

"Okay, you can get in free. Can I text you the address?"

"No, just tell it to me. Give me your number too."

Sol was irritated by how quickly he obliged. She hadn't shown him the slightest interest, but she could see the gears turning in his head, the fantasies unfolding.

"Is your name Charlie?" she asked.

"Yeah, what's your name?"

Leering, she walked backward, away from the fence, swaying her hips and beckoning him onto the court. He sprinted to the entrance then stepped onto the court, slowing to a confident waltz, an erection gleefully pushing through his sweaty gym shorts. Sol stood in place as he approached her, her hips protruding unnaturally, like a damaged action figure. Charlie's swaggy promenading strut continued, his boner leading him forward like a divining rod. Sol held steady, awaiting his arrival.

One punch sufficed. Before Sol could even unclench her fist, Charlie crashed onto the asphalt, his body expanding in all directions like spilled rice on a kitchen floor. "My name's not Angel," she scoffed.

With equal scorn, he looked up at her and sneered. "I bet you'll still be at my party."

"No contest," Kai suddenly announced, shrugging and holding up her broken tennis racket. Sol grimaced. The splintered wires reminded her of Jerry's braces.

CHAPTER 6
JUNE 15
8:17 P.M.
84°F

"ARE YOU SURE THEY'LL BE HERE?" THEO ASKED Apollo, pulling into the long driveway of an extravagant Fayette County house and turning left at a fork.

"They should be," Apollo answered. "Tim said they were headed to a party, and this is the only party happening in this area. Even the barber knew about it," he continued, stroking his smooth head. Theo groaned as he heard Apollo reach toward the dash, turning off the air conditioning. "Why don't you ever ride with the windows down? Even when it's hot, real air is always better," Apollo said.

Keeping his eyes on the driveway, Theo flicked the air conditioning back on, ignoring Apollo's obviously stupid question. "My car, my rules."

"Word. Oh, I meant to tell you, I saw like four people get parts in their head while I was there."

"So? Parts have been back. They're like Lil Wayne."

"Wayne been washed his whole life. I mention it because the parts were all Js. Apparently Insta is really fucking with what we did."

Theo cringed. Although the hacking plan was supposed to be a final "fuck you" to Six Flags, who'd fired him right before the summer started, he was overwhelmed by the reach of his vengeance. Homes had burned down, dogs had died, power lines had been incinerated, and massive pine trees littered the area surrounding the park. The entirety of Stone Mountain was without power and water. He'd tried following the memes for comfort, but between the jokes emerged images of scorched squirrels, fields of dead birds, cars flayed into metal husks. It was strange to party under such grim conditions, to be responsible for so many crises. He felt fortunate not to have heard any audio from the event.

Theo caught up with Apollo, who was already out of the car and just a few feet from the front door. The house looked like an art project. Each floor of its three stories featured a different material: limestone for the first floor, brick for the second floor, and stucco for the third. The different strata of the house were coated in the same warm pink, but the hybrid composition was still apparent. Theo was reminded of his dad's tendency to consciously dress casually when they visited their family in the hood, but to still drive his Mercedes instead of Theo's Civic. Humility always had a threshold.

"Man, what kind of weak party ends before sunset?" Apollo asked, pointing at the empty driveway. "There's not even any lights on."

"Maybe we missed it?" Theo speculated, ringing the doorbell. A middle-aged white woman in pajamas emerged, visibly irate.

"Jesus Christ, you kids can't even fully comprehend a goddamn text message, and those were made for your short-ass attention spans. I wrote the text my damn self, and y'all are still waking me up. Were the directions not clear? The party is in the cluuuuubhoooooouse out back. Park in the paaaaaarking lahhhht. Do you know what a parking lot is? It's not my fucking driveway. Jesus, Lord of Nazareth, you kids." She closed the door.

Theo and Apollo walked back to the car, the moon lighting their path. "Damn, their house has a parking lot," Apollo stuttered.

"Dude, their house has another house," Theo answered. Theo started the car and drove back toward the fork, turning around and going right instead of left. Giant manicured pine trees lined the road leading to the clubhouse, indifferently penetrating the sky.

Theo parked in the filled lot, still in awe of the estate, his jaw limp. The clubhouse was smaller than the main house, but much less humble. Two artificial waterfalls flanked the front door, cascading into shallow pools that were dug into the porch. Even more miraculously, there was no splashing.

o o o

THE HOUSE LACKED BLINDS AND CURTAINS, SO Theo and Apollo had a clear glimpse of the ambient mirth just beyond the door. Postured bodies filled the rooms, their movements bizarrely intentional. This was a pro-flex zone. Surprisingly, no sounds were escaping the party.

Apollo rang the doorbell then stuffed his hands back into his shorts. No one answered. Apollo twisted the doorknob. It was locked. All of this damn open-access opulence and they still managed to lock the door. Apollo didn't feel it was an accident.

"Looks like we finally found a door even the great Apollo can't open," Theo teased, bending forward, arching his back, and erratically moving his fingers, mocking Apollo's typical posture when he typed.

Apollo coughed out a weak laugh then pulled out his phone to call Kai. She didn't answer, but she texted him immediately. "At a party. Zed is still mad at you. Don't call her." Reluctantly, he tried Sol. *She probably doesn't even have my number*, he thought.

"Speak."

"You know who this is?"

"No, I'm just disrespectful to everyone I talk to."

"You know, it's not really sarcasm if it's true."

"What do you want, Apollo? I'm not a fucking operator. If you want to talk to Zed, call her."

"But she won't answer."

The line clicked off. Apollo turned to Theo and shrugged. Theo pounded on the door, his last resort. Moments later, the door swung open, inundating the porch with music and light. A beefy white guy stepped into the doorway, his body so thick that both the light and sound seemed to diminish in his presence.

"Twenty dollars," he announced, crossing his arms.

Apollo sighed, fishing in his pocket for some loose cash. Finding nothing but the fabric of his jeans, he turned to Theo, who nodded with assurance. Theo removed a wad of bills and paid the beefy pseudo-bouncer, who then stepped aside and beckoned them in, closing the door behind them. The party seemed to continue undisturbed, but Apollo knew they'd made an entrance.

He surveyed the large living room. Zed, Sol, and Kai were nowhere to be found. They were probably outside, avoiding the raucous folk music that boomed from hidden speakers. Reluctant to receive any further unwanted attention, he directed Theo to a corner of a stolid dining room, where a few partygoers were huddled over a computer.

Apollo could tell by their conversation that they were the DJs. And he could tell by the fact that there were three of them that they were self-appointed.

"I don't care about how crazy his concerts are. Action Bronson is not party music," a tall redheaded girl insisted. She had thighs like a cheerleader and hair like a country singer. "If you contaminate this queue with another hookless rap song, I'll tell Charlie to make a move on your sister. You know he'll do it."

Her target, a slovenly white guy with a budding beard, stood up and left the room, relinquishing his DJ duties. The redhead began her assault on her other companion, a small Latina with shining, oily skin. She wasn't as pliant.

"This is a party, not a prison experiment. Just play what people like," the small girl said.

"Fuck people. People and their likes are why the radio sucks."

"Your car doesn't even have a radio."

"Yeah, because it sucks. Only idiots listen to the radio."

"Fuck you, Alice," the Latina sighed loudly, grabbing her beer and leaving the room. A new song began playing immediately.

Apollo and Theo glanced at each other, smirks erupting across their face as they both saw a unique opportunity emerging right before their eyes. "Q and Bond?" they asked each other in unison. Theo approached the DJ table as Apollo slinked behind it.

"Can I help you?" Alice asked Apollo.

"Yeah, my phone died. I just need to send an email to my friend who was supposed to meet me here," Apollo answered.

"Make it quick," Alice said, stepping aside.

"Is this Brandi Carlile?" Theo chimed in on cue.

Alice's green eyes immediately flared with interest. "Yes, it is. You listen to her?"

"I used to," Theo purred.

Alice frowned at him, curious yet skeptical. All Theo needed was her curiosity. Continuing to talk her up, he led her away from the DJ table, his eyes secretly meeting Apollo's whenever she took a hearty swig from her beer. By the time Apollo had performed his black magic, Alice was already soliciting bodily contact, her frequent laughs now entailing light taps on Theo's chest or shoulders. Apollo quickly spirited Theo away. This wasn't a night for full Bond.

"I could really see myself with her," Theo confessed with regret as they walked into a large kitchen with slick marble floors and a prairie's worth of counter space.

"You've just got scarlet fever, dude," Apollo said.

"You'd know about fevers, wouldn't you?" Theo joked, picking up a pair of chopsticks from the counter and crudely tapping an Asian riff on the counter. "Scarlet fever, jungle fever, yellow fever. Nothing wrong with getting a little hot. It's been a weird day."

Apollo didn't answer, refusing to take the crudely packaged bait. Theo always got a little cocky when they pulled a Q and Bond. Kai would put him back in his place.

o o o

ZED SAT UP IN HER POOLSIDE CHAIR AND SCANNED the backyard, her eyes sweeping over swaying bodies and immaculately cut grass. Every time Apollo and Theo hijacked a party, T.I.'s "Be Easy" was the first song on their makeshift playlist. Apollo didn't even like the song, but he liked the humor of telling the victims of his petty piracy to be cool about it. Zed found the gesture to be even more obnoxious than usual.

Zed tracked Kai to a circle of skaters standing thirty feet away, circulating a quickly evaporating joint. She looked happy. Zed found Sol on a luxurious inflated chair, lying on her back as she drifted around the pool, her glossy weave shimmering in the moonlight. Both Kai and Sol were thoroughly occupied. *Good,* Zed thought, rising from her chair and heading toward the house. Despite feeling full of purpose, she still managed to walk aimlessly, the party's ambient idleness seeping in. She knew Apollo and Theo would be in the kitchen, which was accessible from the pool, but she took a roundabout route, wandering through the labyrinthine house. All of the doors were locked. Confined to the home's endless hallways, Zed began to wonder if there were more passages than rooms, more arteries than chambers.

One door was completely ajar. Zed slinked in, gawking at the lavish gold-trimmed molding that lined the floor. In the center of the room, some kids crowded around a computer screen. They eagerly beckoned her over.

"Have you seen this?" a tall white girl asked excitedly.

"Seen what?" Zed replied.

"This!" a white boy sporting a crew cut shouted, reloading a YouTube video. A small hole formed in the huddle. Zed stepped in, focusing on the computer screen. The screen was black, but the sound of helicopter propellers was unmistakable. Ten seconds went by. Zed turned and looked at her peers. Their faces were brimming with anticipation, poised for something they knew was coming. Zed pivoted back toward the computer screen. The blackness continued for a full minute then suddenly vanished, a column of light materializing from nowhere, a big bang. Zed continued watching, anxious to see how the video ended. It was clearly footage from the tag. The crew cut boy started to snicker, followed by the tall white girl.

Eventually everyone was laughing, and the light gave way to a picture of Kanye West. "Flashing…lights, lights," everyone in the room started murmuring, backed by the video, which was now sampling the song. "I don't get it," Zed confessed.

"It's just a mash-up video I made making fun of this whole Stone Mountain shit," the boy informed her. "The whole thing is silly. Some asshole just committed arson. It's way more simple than people are allowing it to be. I'm already at four hundred thousand views!"

"So you're saying it's arson when someone carves a letter into a mountain?" Zed asked.

"It was probably already there. Stonewall Jackson is very well-respected in Civil War circles. My dad's into that shit."

Zed immediately left the room, her anger materializing as sweat as she headed toward the kitchen. Theo and Apollo were sweating even harder, dancing in place on gleaming hardwood floors. Zed couldn't recall the name of the dance, but she was sure she'd seen it online. Standing at the edge of the kitchen, she watched their bodies awkwardly jerk, imperiously directed by the thin marionette strings of the dance's savvy inventors. This was a dance that could only be learned through piecemeal imitation, one viral video frame at a time.

"The Kiki!" Zed declared to herself, remembering the dance's name.

"Ki, ki, ki, ki," she watched Apollo chant as he swaggered about, swaying in place while rolling his shoulders back and slapping his upper back. He looked like he was honing a single step of the Macarena. Theo met Zed's eyes then ducked out of the kitchen.

"What are you guys doing here?" Zed asked Apollo, entering the kitchen and placing a firm hand on his shoulder. He immediately stiffened.

"Looking for some friends."

"Did you find them?"

"I think so."

"Did they want to be found?"

"Didn't get to ask."

"Why not?"

"Phone problems."

Zed smirked. Apollo continued. "I saw your tweets. Why are you guys at a party where the host is someone that Sol uppercutted?"

"Are those the only tweets you saw? I'm pretty sure I had a few about my boyfriend who did nothing while his parents treated me like shit."

"I told you my parents were crazy."

"Yeah, but you didn't tell me you'd be such a pushover about it," Zed snapped, storming out of the kitchen and toward the pool.

o o o

APOLLO FOLLOWED HER, BRUSHING PAST GAWKING eyes, Sol's, Theo's, and Kai's among them.

Zed was planted at the edge of the yard, her back to the party and her neck craned upward, moonlight washing over her like a tractor beam. Apollo anchored himself beside her, idly shuffling through his pockets. Still nothing but fabric. Words formed in his mouth but failed to condense outside of it, stifling his thoughts. His hands listlessly scrambled through his pockets. Was he about to get the silent treatment that Kai was always giving to Theo? He hoped not.

Eventually, Zed spoke, her voice calm but still tense. "What was it like up there, Apollo?"

"Where?"

"Space."

"Nothing new. We've looked at Google Earth a bunch of times. You know that. I actually found another available satellite earlier today. Want to look through it later?"

"I didn't ask what it looked like up there. I want to know what it felt like. You weren't just looking at Earth. You had your own giant spray can pointed at it. How'd it feel?"

Apollo spoke immediately. "It was amazing. I never felt that powerful before in my life. It felt like I was doing exactly what I wanted, like pure freedom. It was like tagging, but it didn't feel like it could ever be whitewashed or painted over, you know? It wasn't a giant spray can. It was power. Just power."

"I thought so," Zed briefly replied, her voice trailing off. Another stretch of silence began. The sound of cicadas erupted back into Apollo's ears as if they'd somehow been paused while he and Zed were talking.

Apollo tried to let his mind drift along the crest of the insects' dull drone, escaping into the night, but Zed's mute hostility pulled him right back into the intensity of the moment. Again, the cicadas paused.

"We've got to do it again," Zed announced. Apollo didn't respond.

"We've got to do it again," Zed repeated, her voice lowered further, to a hiss.

"That was a onetime thing, Zed. It can't be repeated. The satellite isn't even showing up online anymore. It's probably been decommissioned. This isn't like Jerry's grave. What we did will be there forever. No one will ever wipe it away."

"No, Apollo, you're wrong. No one knows what happened but us. It doesn't have to be wiped away if no one even sees something to wipe."

"But isn't that what we wanted?"

"Yes, but not like this. We wanted to tag the city, not throw up a billboard! People are already dismissing what happened and making fun of it! 'I Had a Beam' is being used to promote a fucking Major Lazer album! I don't even know who that is, but what the fuck? Even if it's not me being remembered, that's not how I want my work to be remembered. I refuse."

"Calm down. All art gets reused eventually. We can't control how people receive it. You have to let go."

"Don't give me that meme bullshit, Apollo. This isn't the fucking internet where things get a second chance. This is the real world, where things always mean what they will always mean, where arrows fly straight and they either hit the target or they don't. Even if it's just our secret, if we don't change how it's understood right now, it will never mean anything else. Jerry will be a joke to the entire world. And it will have been our fault."

Apollo stared at the moon, contemplating ways to redirect the shame that was bubbling in his gut. *Where are those cicadas when you need them?* He could feel the insects whirring around him, but they were nowhere to be found. In their absence, he found the sounds of Charli XCX. Apollo sighed. Someone had overridden his playlist. He knew he should have used a more complex encryption algorithm. At least this person had taste, though.

His focus returned to Zed, whose back was still turned to him and the party. He wanted to give her an answer, but variables swarmed through his head like maddened ants. Someone could snitch, someone could die, they could kill people, they could get caught, they could be hunted by drones. Apollo shuddered. Was Jerry, someone he hadn't even known about twenty-four hours ago, really worth all that? Why was his so-called legacy so important? All he had seemed to do was be a friend. Was friendship really worth hijacking a military weapon and using it for a tag…again? It felt worth it the first time. The tragedy of Jerry's life spoke to Apollo on a primordial level. He'd enlisted in Theo's crusade against Six Flags, but he was born into Jerry's struggle against the police. How could he turn away from that? How could he turn away from Zed?

Apollo found himself gazing into the moon again. Silently, it stared back at him, offering light but not answers, opaque in its very luminescence.

"I'm down," Apollo stammered, his eyes locked on Zed's back. She turned, her hair swinging over her shoulder like a raised mace. She stepped forward and faced Apollo directly, almost confrontationally. Apollo expected a slap, but received a peck instead, her thin lips slickly gliding across his. Grabbing his left hand, she led him back to the party, where they proceeded to corral their friends. Kai and Theo were sitting poolside, the quiet splashing of their partially submerged legs the only sound between them.

o o o

"Where's Sol?" Zed asked.

"Probably caking. You know how she does," Theo said. "She just understands women, I guess."

"It's not hard," Kai said, removing her legs from the pool, rising, then leaving Theo behind.

After lingering for a moment, Zed and Apollo continued toward the house, hands still clasped as Theo and Kai filed behind them. The party was dying down, its death fueled by a rumor that there was an even better party in Peachtree City. They found Sol on a couch in the living room, curled up like a hermit crab, her shell the chest of Alice, who was also dozing.

"She never talks about juvie, but I feel like this was what probably happened," Kai snorted, inciting a booming collective laugh. "This bitch is over here making literal bosom buddies," Kai continued, summoning a second wave of guffaws. Sol stirred at the sound, dazed yet compliant. She quickly rose, following them out the front door.

After making plans to convene once Waffle House reopened, the crew split up, exchanging hugs and daps and retreating to their cars, which were parked on opposite sides of the lot. Despite the setbacks of the day, both known and unknown, Zed felt there was resolution in the air. *Maybe Sol will finally talk,* she hoped. Kai had told her about the liquor cabinet.

High, but somehow still perceptive, Kai pointed out an object lodged between the windshield wipers of Zed's MINI. Kai grabbed it and read it aloud: "Hey angels I knew you would come to my party. You're welcome, bitches. Je suis Charlie."

"Oh hell nah. You got some paint? I'm gonna tag the shit out of this McMansion motherfucker."

Zed shrugged and climbed into the car, starting it. "Let's just go home," she said. "I promise you we can do something much worse. Trust." Kai laughed and obliged, opening the passenger door and plopping down into the seat. "Fuck Fayette County," Sol declared, folding into the back seat as the car pulled out onto the street, the night taking them in like family.

JULY

AVERAGE HIGH: 89°F

AVERAGE LOW: 71°F

CHAPTER 7
JULY 5
3:12 P.M.
85°F

"What does DC smell like?" Rick asked.

Tilly kept her eyes on the road, pretending she had missed the question. She knew he would ask again, but she had learned to cherish these silent interstices. They didn't happen often.

She never played her music when she drove because Rick always found something to say about it, and although it was inconvenient, moments like this made it worth it.

If it weren't so dangerous to look at Rick directly, to encourage him, she'd steal a glance just to see how happy he was. It was enviable how radiant he looked when his voice was filling a room. Or her damn ear. His mouth would just erupt, his lips spreading like wings, his teeth emerging like a butterfly from chrysalis, a smile pouring forth, transfiguring his entire face. She wished she could smile like that.

Instead, she continued to stare ahead, concentrating on the unending sea of bumpers, the slowest stampede. Most people in the city weren't even off yet, but traffic was thick.

"Did you hear me?" Rick finally asked, concerned.

"Yeah. It doesn't have a smell."

"No smell? I don't believe that! You grew up there, you went to college there, and you worked there. There's gotta be some smell you caught a few times. Cherry blossoms, black squirrels, motorcades, spilled craft beer, chili bowls, bodies in the Potomac. That's gotta smell some type of way!"

"It doesn't have a smell," Tilly said flatly.

"I don't believe you."

"Well, that's on you. I can't tell you what to believe." *Christ,* Tilly thought, *he's dragged me in.*

"That's true, but something I do believe is that this is our case. Like *the* one. You know how every partnership has that one case? Somerset and Mills got the seven deadly sins case. Riggs and Murtaugh got the South African diplomat case. Peretti and Appleton got fucking Nino."

"You know all of those partnerships are fictional, right?"

"Yeah, but that's not important. What's important is that they agreed when they found the one that they were going all the way in. No mercy. Maximum tradecraft."

"Sure. We're not cops, though."

"Damn, that's a good point," Rick said, defeated.

Tilly secretly rejoiced as traffic began to thin out. Escaping from I-20, she merged onto Lee Street, heading south. To her surprise, Rick didn't say anything as they sped past the West End Mall. He usually had a story or five from his days as a janitor there, but he remained silent. *I could get used to this,* Tilly thought.

Eventually they reached the movie studio formerly known as Fort McPherson. A bespectacled black woman greeted them at the security post.

Tilly rolled down the window, wincing as hot air slithered into the car.

"License and affiliation," the guard said gruffly.

Tilly extracted her license and FBI ID from her purse and handed them over. "FBI."

The woman examined the cards closely then shoved them back into the car.

"First right, third left, second lot. You'll know the building when you see it. Don't get lost," the guard warned, retreating back into the post.

Tilly rolled up the window and drove forward.

"Tyler Perry must have opened up a strip club," Rick joked. "The security here is better than ours."

Tilly laughed, extending their stop at the first intersection to regain her composure. "If that were true, we wouldn't be here," she eventually said, easing the car into the first right turn.

The parking lot was empty except for a single unmarked vehicle and a golf cart. Their destination, a solitary brick building, was also unmarked, Tilly noted. No sign or marquee or placard. Maybe it was a movie set. Casually, they strolled into the building.

A balding white man sat at a bare reception desk, his face alert.

"Erickson and Herrington?" he asked, jolting to a stand.

Tilly nodded. The man darted from behind the desk and led them down a short hallway, pivoting into an open doorway in one easy motion. Walking past empty offices, Tilly and Rick shuffled in behind him. The room was windowless and bare, lightly furnished with a giant wooden table and far too many office chairs bunched around it, like pups fighting for their mother's teats. The man closed the door and immediately began speaking.

"Sorry for the rush, but I've only got this conference room for ten minutes. Space is really limited around here."

Discreetly, Tilly kicked one of the empty chairs between them.

"As you know, I'm with Space Command. We protect, deploy, and maintain US government satellite equipment. During last month's incident, Satellite ZX9874 was hijacked and used for unauthorized purposes. Within certain limitations, I have been tasked with helping you find out the means of that breach as well as the perpetrators. Please direct any questions about this satellite toward me, and I will be happy to oblige. Within certain limitations."

Tilly spoke first. "Fantastic. First off, this is embarrassing, but what's your name? Our director tends to be brief in emails, so he didn't mention it."

"Unfortunately, it's classified."

Tilly kicked another chair.

"So, how is this even possible?" Rick asked. "How does a satellite that's so strategically important get hacked?"

"I can't speak to whether it is strategically important or not, but this happened solely due to the nature of this satellite. When this former base was decommissioned and sold, some of the infrastructure was left intact due to security reasons that I'm not at liberty to discuss. Moving or rebuilding that infrastructure would have been extremely costly."

"More costly than a national monument and surrounding neighborhoods being destroyed?" Tilly bristled.

"Terrorism is not a line item on the Space Command budget," he dryly replied. "And monuments and neighborhoods can be rebuilt. The kind of infrastructure that enables a satellite of this caliber isn't a matter of just unplugging some computers and uploading data to *the cloud*."

Tilly glowered. People loved to use "the cloud" as a whipping boy, as if it were any more nebulous than "space" on a hard drive the size of a thumb or "visiting" a web page.

Rick jumped in. "Okay, sure, this satellite has some unique circumstances, but in terms of personnel, who is capable of this? Do you have a watch list or anything? Particular countries, organizations, individuals?"

"Yes, but that's classified."

Tilly sighed. Was this what big cases were like? Evasions on top of elisions on top of elusions? Maybe she should have been a journalist. Then she'd at least be able to get away with a write-around, using the gaps as an indictment.

"Are there any recordings from the night of the incident?" she asked him.

"No, unfortunately."

"Are there any technical logs or digital signatures that you can provide?"

"Not that I can provide, sorry."

"So, what can you tell us?" Tilly finally relented.

"All I have for you two is career advice. For cases like this, you just have to roll with what you're given. I understand that you care about your job and that you have values and want to get out here and solve this, but the people who stick around aren't the people who solve every piece of the case. The people who stick around are the ones who take the little they got and make something from it. So don't look at me like I'm the reason you don't have any perps. The play don't care who makes it."

Before Tilly could respond, a dull knock drifted through the room. The balding man rose immediately, gesturing at the door. Tilly shot up just as quickly, exiting without a word. The hallway was filled with people, but Tilly avoided their eyes, making a beeline to the parking lot.

Rick joined her soon after, oddly stoked.

"Why are you smiling? Did you finally get that asshole to open up?" Tilly asked him.

"Nah, Angela Bassett was in the hallway. You walked right past her. She's working with some screenwriters on a script for a *Stella* reboot."

Tilly chortled. At least the man had been honest about the conference room. That didn't explain why the parking lot was still empty, but there were more pressing problems.

Silently, Tilly and Rick sauntered to her car, both of them opening the doors and lingering outside to let the hot air filter out. The tan leather would still be molten, but that couldn't be fixed. After a spell, they slid in.

"Within certain limitations," Rick said as they exited the base, "I think we'll be all right."

"You listen to too much Kendrick Lamar. We're fucked."

"No such thing as too much Kendrick. And yes, we are fucked, but that's not necessarily a bad thing. The guy was kind of right. We won't be able to solve this case, but we can build a case."

"You're not telling me anything I don't already know."

"Exactly. If there isn't a trail to follow, you build a trail."

"You sound like you're giving a Ted Talk."

"Not all of them are bad."

Rick continued, but Tilly stopped listening, focusing on the road ahead. Somehow, she was supposed to solve a cybercrime without the help of the government agency affected and without access to the digital scene of the crime. Maybe the higher-ups really were trying to shut down the Atlanta office.

Suddenly exhausted, she realized she needed a shutdown herself. Or a restart. They never worked one case at a time. There had to be something with some loose ends.

"Hey," she said softly, "where are we at on that Sims case?"

"Still waiting on him to do something stupid. Shouldn't take too long, considering his MO, but we're tied up until he moves."

"Damn. How about the aquarium case? Haven't heard about that in a while."

"We closed it in June."

"Councilman Lanza? That goes to trial soon."

"Was supposed to start later this month, but the prosecutor offered a plea deal. She bought a cruise ticket for September. She'd have had to push it back if she'd presented all the evidence we gave her."

"Shit."

Tilly had missed the slight turn to continue onto Lee, back toward I-20 and rush hour. It could easily be corrected, but she hated U-turns. Defiantly, she remained on Whitehall, a slight sense of subversion rising in her as the car ducked under I-20.

"I don't feel like working this case right now," she confessed after a few minutes of silence. "Take me somewhere I haven't been before."

"You sure?"

Tilly knew he was warning her, but she'd do anything not to end up back at home, telling herself she was relaxing just because she was listening to Drake and reviewing case files in her pajamas.

"Yeah."

"Bet!" he exclaimed. "Left on Forsyth," he said seconds later. As soon as they'd turned, he pointed to a lot on the left.

Tilly pulled in, parking in the back next to a lemon-yellow Suburban with shimmering black trim. The other cars in the lot were just as customized, a Candyland for a Toretto or an O'Conner.

"Leave your phone," Rick told her before they stepped out the car.

"Leave your gun," she replied back, disarming herself.

So, this was the legendary Magic City, the strip club where rappers nationwide came to jettison their money. It didn't look like much, Tilly thought. They approached a windowless rectangular building, a blocky citadel with the squat dimensions of a brick. When she'd moved to Atlanta, all her girlfriends in DC had joked she'd secretly been hired here. "People move to Atlanta for two reasons," Nikki told her the night before she moved. "More money and more space." Maybe she'd put in an application, Tilly thought, if that was how strip clubs even worked. She'd have to ask just for kicks, she decided as they neared the entrance. This place was always coming up in cases anyway. There had to be something going on.

"Don't even think about it," Rick warned when they reached the door. She tended to grimace when she was thinking about casework. "This is pleasure, not business."

Tilly scowled, slinking into the empty line for security. Two dozy guards patted them down then waved them off. Tilly was surprised by their professionalism. They checked everywhere.

Inside, there was just enough light to discern various bodies, but only when they were in motion. She knew they were mostly men. That was guaranteed. Rick was saying something, but Tilly struggled to hear him over the sounds of some Rihanna song that her body knew but her mind didn't recognize. Something about working. Was Rihanna stressed or liberated? The fact that Tilly even had to ask made her feel old.

"What?!" she eventually shouted at Rick.

"Are you hungry?" he shouted back, finally audible. Extending his arm, he guided her into a seat near an empty, unlit stage.

"Yeah, I am."

"The chicken and waffles is pretty good," he advised, settling down a seat away.

A lean server dressed in black lingerie appeared soon after, taking their orders. Tilly surprised herself when she ordered a cocktail. Rick ordered coffee. Instinctively, Tilly scanned the room as the woman walked away. An unfathomable pile of money was forming beneath a gyrating dancer on another stage, all provided by one man. Tilly wondered if the waitstaff had a tip out arrangement with the dancers. In such a clearly hierarchical environment, it had to be competitive. There were probably weekly fights. High turnover. Cliques. Alliances. Spies.

"You're doing it again," Rick warned her, wrinkling up his face in mockery. "We're not always on the clock."

The cocktail arrived quickly. Tilly hesitated to drink it. Was she really about to drink on a Wednesday afternoon, with a coworker, in a strip club? She'd been to a million happy hours, but this was something else.

Abruptly, the stage in front of her lit up. Vibrant hues of amethyst and sapphire snaked around the stage's towering pole. Coolly, a woman appeared, as thick as a pillar, curves like an orbit. Her strut was spectacular, each step made to be remembered. She channeled rhythm like a conduit, her wide hips swaying slowly. She mounted the pole legs first, defying physics by sliding up before easing down. Before her feet touched the ground, cash began to swarm around her, gliding across her gleaming, quivering skin, the smoothest transaction. The woman had a supernatural relationship with the booming music, Tilly felt, her fleshy body dissolving into the flickering stage lights, every jiggle eerily deliberate, every dollar earned.

Tilly sipped her drink.

CHAPTER 8
JULY 17
11:31 A.M.
87°F

THE JULY SUN HAMMERED INTO KAI'S BACK AS SHE jumped rope in her driveway. She hated the purity of jumping rope. It could never be anything other than straight up work, no matter how much you tried to make it fun. Kai had tried everything, but nothing ever worked: headphones always fell out, speakers got drowned out by the slap of the rope against the concrete, and it was never scenic because it could only be done in one place. Jump roping was labor through and through, no breaks, no daydreaming, no thrills, just calories evaporating into the ether.

It worked, though. After thirty-five minutes, Kai felt the same level of exhaustion as after an hour of tennis. Satisfied, she stopped, tossing the nylon rope aside and plopping into the gasping crabgrass of her front yard.

June was gone forever, along with her interest in Theo. He'd spent an entire month hounding her about what they'd done and complaining about the heat. She could deal with the latter, but the former was unexpected. How could he have had such a drastic change of a heart about a plan he'd cooked up? They'd tagged schools and hospitals and houses and businesses and cars and headstones. He knew how collateral damage worked. This was graffiti, not a gluten-free bake sale. Maybe his hatred for Six Flags had blinded him, Kai considered. He hated that place so much that he'd once rear-ended someone on I-20 because he was too distracted throwing the theme park a double finger. Whatever the case, she didn't care. They were over.

Good thing she'd decided to go to a school he hadn't applied to, unlike Zed and Apollo, who were both going to Georgia Tech. They seemed good, though; they could stick it out. Her and Theo? Nah.

Sprawling out on the prickly grass, Kai exhaled, more defeated than fatigued. After two weeks of declined invitations, she'd finally gotten Sol to commit to tennis, but this morning, the day they were supposed to meet, the chick had still managed to cancel, citing a recent adjustment to her work schedule. Kai scoffed at the thought. Sol's Waffle House could have been staffed by a team of actual waffles. It got so little business during the day that Sol and Kai had once rolled a joint at a table, smoked it, fell asleep, woke up, fell asleep again, woke up again, Febreezed the entire restaurant, and then waited around for another two hours before any customers came. That bitch wasn't working.

Kai bolted up, trotting to her open garage. Her meager transit options stared back at her: bike, skateboard, worn Asics. Theo's busted Civic briefly felt like an Escalade.

Kai chose the bike. A few hills later, she was frantically pedaling down State Route 314, receiving ambiguous honks and shouts as cars veered around her. Was she being hit on or being warned she'd get hit? Kai wasn't sure, but these drivers were stressing her out. She couldn't wait to get to Old National so she could ride on the sidewalk. Wow, was she actually *looking forward* to going to Old National? That was a first.

Seconds after she turned onto Flat Shoals Road, a rowdy Corolla nearly made contact with her back tire. "The street is not a bike lane, boo-boo!" the driver, a spectacled older black woman, informed her. Kai agreed, banking onto Castlegate Drive, a side street. She wasn't about to battle over the road in the midday sun. Changing plans as she rolled down Castlegate, she decided to go to Sol's house, near Godby Road. If Sol was there, she'd crash and talk to her one-on-one. If not, she'd go home, turn on the air conditioning, and try to hit the lottery with another tennis invitation. It wasn't a solid plan, but when the sun was this relentless, liquid, gas, and plasma weren't so bad.

Worn duplexes decayed in real time as Kai sped through Castlegate. She exited the neighborhood just as quickly as she'd come, drifting into a nameless residential strip with refreshingly empty streets. Fifteen minutes later, she was creaking across Sol's front porch, sweat surging down her face. *Sol better have something good to drink, even that awful-ass tea,* Kai thought, extending her sweaty arms to ring the doorbell. No answer.

She rang it again.

Nothing.

Flustered, Kai turned and scowled at Sol's re-stolen bike, which was parked in the front yard.

"I know you're in there!" she shouted, thumping on the glass storm door with her open palm, its hot glass irritating her skin. The door leered back at her, unfazed.

She thumped harder. "Come on, girl! It's hotter than a Baptist revival out here! Stop playing around!" she protested. "You can at least give me some tea!"

Exhausted, Kai leaned forward, pressing her forehead to the storm door. The trip back was going to be unpleasant at best. She had to stop leaving the house without cash.

"Bitch, do I look like a zoo animal?" Sol joked, opening her front door and unlatching the door. "Niggas think that just because they knock on glass, a bitch is supposed to do flips and wave."

"Well, you were in a cage once," Kai retorted, stepping into the house. Sol sneered, closing the door and heading to the kitchen. Kai remained in the living room, staring up in disbelief. Elaine, the name of Sol's grandmother, was tagged all over the ceiling. The strokes were messy and unstylized, some real amateur shit.

"Do you really want tea, or were you just hitting me with the kryptonite?" Sol asked from the kitchen.

"I'll take anything."

"Tea it is."

Kai watched as Sol poured the glass slowly, deliberately, a technician at work. Masterfully, she left room for ice then grabbed the glass and tenderly pressed the ice dispenser embedded in the fridge. The ice tumbled down without a single splash. She was good. She'd probably been pouring a lot of drinks lately, Kai realized.

Kai left the kitchen, diving into the couch, her neck parallel with the seat, her arms spread wide like she was hugging a bookshelf.

"What do you want?" Sol demanded, standing over Kai.

"I want a few things. First, I really want that tea."

Sol obliged, handing over the glass. Kai shot up, taking the glass and promptly emptying it down her throat.

"Second, I need you to talk."

"Talk about what?"

"About this," Kai said, gesturing at torn drywall, ripped carpet, gutted wires jutting out of the wall, and, of course, that ceiling. "You opening a skate park?"

"No, but I'm getting rid of this dump."

"Are you crazy? This house is great."

"It's all right. I can do better."

"Better than a paid off house at eighteen? Just a month ago, you were talking about how cheap you're living and about how the next round of improvements will be some HGTV shit. What happened?"

"I called my parents every day after Derrick came by, and they haven't answered a single fucking time."

"Not once?"

"Not twice either."

"That doesn't necessarily mean anything."

"I know. That's the problem."

"So how does that make you feel?"

"I'm not talking about this."

"Your call. Well, let's talk about how you keep blowing me off."

"What's there to talk about?"

"Solara, stop fucking around. I'm really trying to figure out what's up with you. I haven't seen you since you randomly punched out that white kid, you keep Instagramming pictures of you and Antonio, who I know you only hang out with to score booze, and you keep looking out the window like a damn worried dog. Girl, what is going on?"

∘ ∘ ∘

SOL STARED AT KAI, TACITURN. IN JUVIE, THE counselors had always blabbered about the importance of "emotional transparency." Sol could still remember the way Ms. Watts, the head counselor, would slowly and loudly pronounce the latter word. "Trans-PAAARENNNNCYYY," she'd croon, as if she were teaching toddlers. The counselors had always seemed to neglect the fact that they were teaching in a jail, a place where all emotions were liable to be used against you. Sol didn't fault them—of course the theories seemed true when jail was your nine-to-five instead of your midnight-to-midnight—but she stopped listening after the first week.

This choice had served her well. Unlike her second cellmate, Patricia Frauland, a stocky blond white girl with a concrete jaw and eyes the size of beads, she'd never gotten extorted. Personal information was currency in juvie, and Sol had been so tight-lipped that she wasn't even listed at the currency exchange. Patricia, on the other hand, was constantly filing for bankruptcy. Every week, she acquired a new best friend. And every other week, one of those friends acquired a brutal thrashing after leaking a choice secret or two. Sol laughed.

Kai stared at her. "Is there something I should know, or are you just not talking about yourself at all?"

Sol stood up and fanned herself with the bottom of her oversized T-shirt. "Walk with me," she said. "It's hot in here."

Kai rose, trailing Sol into the kitchen, where they leaned against the counters on opposite sides of the room. Sol removed a glass from a cabinet and reached into the refrigerator, grabbing the tea pitcher. "You want some more?" she asked.

"Yeah, this is actually really fucking good."

"I've been trying to tell everyone that it's never been bad! I just made one bad batch one time, when everybody happened to be over. And y'all niggas just agreed that the shit had always been bad, ole anti-statistical asses."

Kai cackled, doubling over yet holding her glass out to be replenished.

Sol emptied the pitcher then poured herself a glass of wine using a bottle she'd left on the counter. The bottle was depleted before her glass was even half full.

"Sorry to have been off the map," she said. "It's just been hard. No one in my family has helped with the transition from juvie to normal life. My uncle drove me here and used to come see me a few times a week, but that's it. My family treats me like I'm a career criminal. Derrick came over last month and tried to sneak in the house. I don't have the fucking slightest what he was up to. I scared him off, but he probably went back and told everybody else how I threatened him. And I know I shouldn't care because fuck them, but I do. All year, I took care of this house because I thought if I showed them what I had done with it, and showed them what I'd done with myself by graduating on time, they would at least talk to me. But after Derrick was over here, it just seemed useless. When I told him I owned the house, he looked at me like I was just trash. So now I've trashed the house… Stupid, I know."

Kai nodded sympathetically. "Wow, that's like the realest shit you've ever told me. This is like some best friend shit," she whispered.

"Jesus Christ, you're a fucking corn dog."

"Hell yeah. Hot, brown, salty, and popular among the lazy and degenerate."

"You know I just poured my fucking soul out to you, right?"

"Yeah, I know. Felt good, right?"

"Not really. Don't you have anything better to do than to solve my problems?"

"Yes. But I'm doing it anyway, so first, I need you to make more tea. Second, give me the booze so I can flush it. Third, I don't really know. Zed and Apollo will explain the rest. Just know that there are more satellites. Lots more. Let's smoke."

"Okay," Sol replied, shuffling through the cabinet for a pot to boil some water. Finding one, she filled it and placed it on the stove. Kai trailed her as she traipsed over to the liquor cabinet. Did she really have to throw all that liquor away?

"Yes," Kai's stern face answered. Sighing, Sol forked over three bottles of tequila and a bottle of whiskey. Kai beamed with satisfaction, retrieving Sol's wine glass from the kitchen counter then heading to the bathroom.

Sol remained in the living room, plopping onto the couch and surveying the destruction she'd wrought over the last month. The carpet was stained red from cheap merlot. The fan hung limply from the ceiling, spinning like a skipped record. Her grandmother's couch smelled of blunt ashes and corn syrup.

This house—Sol's house—didn't deserve this. Training her eyes on the ceiling, she tried to ask her grandmother for forgiveness, her body unwinding as her few sips of wine churned in her empty stomach.

Her spirit was uneasy. Something didn't feel right. She paused, focusing on the sound of liquids draining into her toilet bowl, thick yet smooth. Each splash hit her like a pinprick, irking her, nudging her toward the truth.

She didn't want her grandmother to forgive her. What she wanted was for her grandmother to look away. She wanted another drink.

CHAPTER 9
JULY 21
10:13 A.M.
86°F

MR. PANG'S HANDS LEFT THE STEERING WHEEL FOR the fourth time in two minutes. Apollo had never seen him this frustrated.

"I told you we should have taken MARTA, Dad," Zed taunted.

"But the GPS said traffic was light, and why drive somewhere, park, take a train, then *walk*, when I can skip one step?" Mr. Pang argued.

"You're only skipping one step, Dad, and you're not even skipping it. You're replacing it with rush hour traffic."

"Well it's still not my fault. Who schedules an orientation at 11 a.m. on a Monday?"

Apollo nodded, agreeing with them both but not intervening. He'd never seen Zed's family speak above an excited whisper. It was refreshing to see that they too weren't above yelling. Plus, he hated MARTA in the morning: legions of aspiring rappers, stressed young moms, condescending yuppies, shook white suburbanites, indignant homeless people, and tired working folks, all packed into blocky seats with poorly placed handrails and a color scheme straight out of an art class for preteen moms. Apollo wasn't too good to ride MARTA, but he knew it too well to be anything other than ambivalent.

His eyes floated to a nearby car that they'd been parallel with for almost half a mile. A suited black woman sat in the driver's seat of a Subaru Outback, her windows rolled down, an Erykah Badu song leaking out. She was sweating profusely. Traffic was exercise.

"If you think this is bad, wait until we try to look for parking," Zed goaded.

"Zadie, why do you insist on being so pessimistic?"

"Zed, Dad. I'm not being pessimistic, I just wish you would listen to me. I drive into the city all the time. You drive *around* the city all the time. I know a few things."

"Hmm," Mr. Pang replied, polite but dismissive.

Apollo abandoned their conversation. There was too much traffic ahead for it to continue to be entertaining.

Two miles and one half hour later, they were on the outskirts of Georgia Tech, searching for Mr. Pang's mythical parking spot. Although it took ten minutes of circling the block, the legend turned out to be true. Parking in front of the Waffle House on Fifth Street, they hopped out and hustled into the heart of Georgia Tech's campus. Mr. Pang hated being late.

"Williams Street!" Mr. Pang exclaimed as they crossed over I-85, their pace undisturbed.

"What's so important about Williams Street?" Apollo asked. "Thinking about opening another restaurant?"

"No! That's the home of Adult Swim!" Mr. Pang answered with a tone of obviousness.

Apollo grinned and continued following Zed, who was leading. Mr. Pang was so cool. Well, maybe, Apollo reconsidered. *He probably just watches Family Guy,* Apollo decided, declining to verify. He liked his categories to remain stable.

"Where are we headed, Zadie?" Mr. Pang asked.

"Zed! Zed!" she yelled. A group of startled students gawked from the front yard of a Greek dormitory. Apollo found their matching T-shirts to be uniquely embarrassing. They looked like a successful dodgeball team: triumphant, but united in uncoolness.

Mr. Pang sighed, speaking slowly. "Where are we going, Zed?" The "d" in her name was noticeably blunt, offensively percussive.

"The Ferst Art Center," she said, cloyingly pleasant.

"Where is that?"

"About ten minutes away."

"Christ."

"Dad, it's just walking. You'll survive."

Mr. Pang sighed and continued forward. The campus designers clearly didn't believe in grids. After banking left down Techwood and winding down Fourth Street, passing students and filled parking spaces and manicured greenery, they found other conspicuously lost first-year families and filed behind them, proceeding to the Ferst building.

Entering the building, Apollo felt overwhelmed as they were herded into a swank auditorium with cozy red seats. From the door to his chair, he had received a pencil, a mug, a ream of glossy brochures, a T-shirt, a pin, and at least four high fives, none of them solicited. Why was college so welcoming?

The room filled quickly as families continued to arrive, their voices incrementally escalating to cut through the loud, ambient chatter. Apollo struggled to hear Zed, who was whispering to him about potential majors. It took him a full minute to realize she was actually shouting.

"How can they call it the College of Computing when they only have two majors?" she asked.

Apollo shrugged, suddenly distracted by movement on the stage. Two young white women in gray pantsuits mounted it calmly, one sitting down in a chair near the edge of the stage and the other walking to the center. The arms of one of the women shot up then slowly descended, adjusting the volume. A few resilient pockets of noise held out, but they were quickly snuffed by an explosion of *shhs* that came from all across the room. Her pantsuit was fitted and spectacularly crisp, each line and edge starched into a spike.

"Quiet, a white woman is speaking," Zed whispered into his ear, making Apollo vomit out a shrill laugh. He was shunned so quickly and decisively that his laugh didn't even stretch past one syllable. Stalling out, his mouth remained agape, his eyes down. *Maybe welcoming isn't the right word,* he thought.

The woman spoke of bland topics like advisors and roommate assignments and the campus bookstore, but her voice was enthralling. Every other sentence was a compliment. Zed and Apollo's class was the biggest, the most competitive, the most diverse, the most international, the most global. Superlatives bounced around the room like a JezzBall, transforming even mundane statements into reasons to applaud. The excitement caused the volume to slowly begin to return to its earlier high, but the woman seemed to be in control, her arms gradually ascending as compliments continued to gush from her perfect, gleaming teeth.

Things really livened once the speech became individualized. "We had a 13 percent acceptance rate this year, but YOU made it! We had the highest average SAT scores on record, but YOU made it. We scheduled this orientation at 11 a.m. on a Monday, but YOU MADE IT." Suddenly, the room detonated, cheers and claps and whistles erupting from nearly every person in attendance. Only the custodian, a small Latino standing near the door with a broom, seemed unfazed. Apollo scoffed when he realized he was also standing; he didn't even remember rising. He looked at Zed, who was also coming down from the collective high. Of all the parents in the audience, only Mr. Pang seemed unaffected; still seated, his legs were indifferently crossed, his brow flat.

As the cheering receded and butts collapsed back into seats, the second woman, whose pantsuit was much looser, rose and elaborated on the topics the first woman had packaged with filler. Her voice was pleasant, but she offered no compliments. Apollo could feel the room drift into hostility. Did this woman not know who she was talking to? They were the class of 2023—disruptors, innovators, pioneers, dreamers. Cell phones gradually migrated to eager hands, crushing candy, snapping selfies. The woman droned on for a solid twenty minutes, losing the audience with each word. But toward the end of her speech, she mentioned football, and the odds were immediately in her favor. One man dropped his phone, the resulting *thunk* echoing throughout the suddenly quiet room.

The speech ended without further mention of football, but the opportunity was not lost. As soon as the second woman turned to head to her seat, the first woman quickly returned, flanked by cheerleaders with gun-like devices. "I heard you guys like football!" Apollo heard her shout as Mr. Pang spirited them out of the auditorium. A towel whizzed over his head into the arms of a small Asian toddler as they rushed down the aisle. Apollo was shocked at how many evil glares the girl received. *Nothing in this world is free,* he heard his mom say from somewhere deep in his skull.

The art center's main hall offered no respite from the grand welcome. Representatives of various student organizations lined the walls, a sea of tables and enthusiasm. Apollo braced himself, wading out into the center of the hall, hoping equidistance would make him invisible. Zed trailed behind him, her sandals dragging on the floor. Apollo welcomed her. Together, they would escape this madness.

They couldn't, Apollo quickly realized. Their early departure from the welcome speeches had marred them. They were the only ones in the hall. Recruitment was their destiny. Within seconds, Zed was lured in by the free sweatpants offered by Blue Cross, Blue Screen, a Christian programming club. Apollo quietly absconded, but then found himself at the table for the 1500 Club. The club, represented by three austere white guys, was mysterious. Their table was covered in a black cloth, but the surface was bare; they didn't even have flyers. The eyes of each rep were hidden behind a pair of hideous transition lenses, the frames of their glasses embarrassingly pedestrian, clearly bought either on sale or in absentia, likely by their mothers.

"What are you guys about?" Apollo asked.

"We all have SAT scores of 1550 or higher," one of them answered.

"Why?"

"Why were our scores high, or why do we unite because of our scores?" another answered. Apollo knew that a different one had spoken, but he couldn't bring himself to look at them directly. They were boring, existentially.

"Why are you a group?" he asked, eyeing other tables over his shoulder.

"Smart people just belong together," the first one told him.

"Guess I won't be joining you then," Apollo said, shirking off. *Kai would have appreciated that burn,* he thought, eager to tell Zed.

"Did you get 1550 or higher?" someone shouted from behind Apollo.

"I got into college," he replied under his breath.

He eventually found himself in front of the table for the African American Student Union. The organization was represented by two black girls, both clad in jeans and black T-shirts emblazoned with AASA, stylized in green, red, and black letters.

"Are you guys Pan-Africanists?" Apollo asked, worried.

"No, we just haven't updated this T-shirt in like twenty years. We've been off that multicultural Kumbaya shit for a minute, though," one of the girls informed him in a casual drawl. "I'm Cherise," she added, offering a handshake. Apollo accepted. Her grip was firm. She reminded him of Sol.

"I'm Apollo," he replied.

"Apollo, please do not let this hooligan ruin your impression of our organization," the other girl interjected in a nasally tone. "The rest of us have home training."

Apollo laughed, unsure how to respond. "So, what do you do?" he inquired.

"We're just black in public," Cherise answered, making Apollo snicker and the other girl frown. "Seriously," she continued, "we exist just because we can. Some of us do other stuff with Black Lives Matter and other larger organizations, but AASU is like Al

Sharpton. We're around because we've been around, not because we *need* to be around, you feel me?"

Apollo nodded, trying not to laugh in the face of the other girl, whose cheeks were turning an ornery red.

"This is not recruitment, Cherise!" the girl exclaimed. "If you think we're so backwards, why do you come to the meetings? Why do you pay the dues? Why are you here over the summer, recruiting?"

"Because allegiance isn't delusion," Apollo jumped in, happy to find a kindred spirit.

"Because things can change," Cherise corrected him. "Including me."

The girl seemed satisfied, but Apollo felt betrayed. "But what if they can't?"

"Even if they can't, there's levels to this shit. Not everyone can be out in the streets or on the highway or in the classroom, but everyone has to keep in contact. Because the moment we think our one battlefield is the entire war, we lose."

"But aren't some battles more important than others?"

Cherise's face shifted in multiple directions, her mind processing his question. "Nigga, I'm not your spiritual advisor," she said after a spell. "Figure that shit out on your own. Just don't be reckless out here, sabotaging other people's battles on some Blue Lives Matter or class first shit." Then she left.

Apollo stood with the other girl, who remained silent. She offered him a pen and pointed toward a mostly empty spreadsheet that was lying on the table.

Apollo wondered how she would have recruited him as he leaned over, considering whether he really wanted to join AASU. Cherise seemed cool, but her politics unsettled him. She had all the same dispositions as him but didn't seem to come to the same conclusions. He glared at the list, indignant. Only one name was scrawled in: Zed Pang.

Apollo didn't sign. He didn't need an organization, especially one that didn't prioritize countering government surveillance and secrecy. Even Solara's thick head understood what was at stake. He'd have to convince Zed to renege, he decided as he reached the end of the hall. They were too woke for such middling affiliations.

There were no more tables to investigate, so Apollo turned and watched the growing activity in the hall, which was becoming densely packed as families streamed out of the auditorium. Zed waved at him from a few yards away, pointing at a table to signal that she was still browsing. Apollo smiled back, mouthing "Take your time" and sitting cross-legged on the wooden floor. He never refused solace.

Ten minutes later, she was finished and plopped down next to him, her spoils crumpled beside her. Apollo kissed her aggressively, eager for a taste of the familiar. Zed laughed in response, pulling away and taunting him before finally allowing him to score another peck.

"Make any enemies?" he asked.

"Maybe. There's some group called the Encrypts. Great name, but all they do is study cryptocurrencies. I told them they're wasting their time."

"And a great name. What's with white guys and cryptocurrencies?"

"Beats me."

"I saw you signed up for the African American Student Union."

"Yeah, they seemed pretty cool."

"Meh. Seemed like they lacked focus to me. 'Let's get together 'cause we're black' is so backwards. There's much better reasons to be getting together."

"You're too smart to really believe that's why they exist, but just in case you do, I'm definitely dragging you to their meetings."

"Whatever."

Mr. Pang suddenly appeared, his face brimming with amusement. Zed and Apollo looked up at him in unison, remaining seated.

"All you two did was walk down a hallway and talk to people. How can you be so tired?"

"Talking is exhausting when no one is listening," Apollo complained.

"I thought everyone was pretty attentive, actually," Zed replied.

Apollo shrugged, grabbing his assorted loot and standing up.

"The meter has two more hours left," Mr. Pang informed them. "I refilled it while you were gone. You two can meet your interim advisors or we can walk around the city, maybe go to the Varsity! It's up to you."

"So that's what that auditorium thing was about? We can just email our advisors. We're not really dressed for meetings."

Mr. Pang's brow slowly lifted. Apollo could feel his gaze linger over his exposed arms, which housed two pound signs inked into his triceps. Suddenly embarrassed, Apollo refracted the glance onto the other new students filling the hall. Almost all of the guys were wearing polos and khakis, and almost all of the girls were clad in floral sundresses. Apollo was the only one rocking a sleeveless tank top, he realized with regret. He hated it when he felt the need to surveil himself. Zed fit in much better, her burgundy sundress compromised only by her knee-length white socks.

"Mm-hmm," was Mr. Pang's only response.

"I want to go home and get back to summer," Zed said, comforting Apollo with a conspiratorial side-eye. "And Dad, the Varsity is gross. Even the soda has grease."

Apollo chuckled, helping Zed up. Mr. Pang sighed and led them out of the building. Outside, they were greeted by blistering heat, sunlight so concentrated that it felt personal, air so humid that Apollo could grasp it in his hand. Summer was overrated.

"I'd like to apologize," Mr. Pang said as they pulled into Apollo's driveway, snapping Apollo awake.

"For what, Dad?"

"Well, I took you guys out of the auditorium because I was annoyed at how big football seemed to be, and that isn't fair to you. It's okay to like football and rallies and organizations and all that other festive college stuff. College is your chance to give new things a shot. Just don't lose yourselves. Sometimes you just have to stick to what you know, okay?"

"Yeah, yeah, yeah, Dad, we'll only try coke. No meth or molly. Please stop."

"Zed, leave him alone. I feel you, Mr. Pang. No worries about us. We've got big plans, and nothing can stop them, not even the wonderful vices of college."

Apollo hopped out of the car, pleased with his answer and hoping Mr. Pang didn't think they really did coke. Apollo had always been warmly received by Zed's family, but he was never sure if they were just polite or if they truly liked him. Apollo seemed to detect a hint of pride on Mr. Pang's face as the car reversed out the driveway, but a glare on the windshield obscured his view.

Apollo's house was empty, but his email inbox was full. Absentmindedly, he scrolled through it, jumping with delight when he read a message from his contact at Google Atlanta. Contacting a janitor actually was a pretty smart move, he realized. Solara was brighter than he'd allowed her to be, he considered, almost thrilled when he could think of no objection to this new thought.

He stood in place, amazed that it was really happening. Not only had Zed found more satellites with lax security, but right here, in his city, there was a supercomputer that could process the complex aerodynamics that were needed to actually reposition the satellites rather than just access their motherboards. They'd have to determine the satellites' orbits, but that would be easy. Right now, all Apollo could think about was his purpose. He restated the facts, too thrilled to think further. In addition to there being *multiple* weaponized satellites, some were less guarded than others, and *he* would hack them. Small world.

His world history professor, Ms. Zarri, had always insisted that war was a competition of logistics—supply management. Weapons and tactics and information mattered, she taught, but only to the extent that they were expertly managed.

Fuck that, Apollo thought. In the US's war against whoever the war was against, there seemed to be a lot more supplies than management. And he was going to show why that was a problem.

He suddenly wished he could rewrite his final term paper for his world history class, which had received an underwhelming B+. Zarri would shit a brick.

The wish petered out when he realized he had no way of confirming his sources. First person is for bloggers and shit journalists, Ms. Zarri had once said. That same day, Apollo had looked her up online. Ms. Zarri was a prolific vlogger, specializing in "investigations" of hair products, according to the video descriptions. There usually wasn't much investigating going on, though, just a cursory Google search, filmed, followed by at least fifteen minutes of sycophantic endorsement or merciless critique. Apollo never brought it up.

Pouncing onto his bed and lying on his stomach, he thought of Cherise. So perfect, yet so flawed. Grabbing his laptop, he decided to look her up. Her

Twitter page was the first result, followed by her blog. He clicked on the blog, perusing her archives. Most of the posts were images, making it easy to navigate. She seemed to go to a lot of rallies. End homelessness. Fuck the police. Citizens first. Save Syria. No GMO. Stop Zionists. Net neutrality. She had a picket sign, and a selfie broadcasting that sign, for every occasion, every objective. It was confusing, Apollo thought. All this awareness, yet she was hanging with AASU, an obviously feeble organization. And Zed wanted to join too. What a joke.

He moved to her Twitter page. It overflowed with retweets, all just as buckshot as her blog. Multitasking and politics never go together, he had read somewhere. You choose one mission, you complete it, then you move on. How did people not get that? He hadn't even had to read that to understand it. Seeing it written just confirmed it.

Apollo rolled onto his back, his eyes resting on the ceiling. It was only 2:30 p.m. There was enough day remaining to get into anything, but he felt immobilized. If this next plan didn't go right, he could end up just like Cherise, satisfied with merely being black in public, fossilized in the exigencies of 1961. Was there any mindset less Jurassic, less reptilian, less basic? It was repulsive how stupid people could be, even smart people. Even Zed. He'd have to make it obvious, for everyone.

Suddenly drowsy, Apollo took refuge in his thoughts, drifting into sleep. He saw the big picture. He'd seen it for himself, on that screen, on that night.

But he was the only one, he realized, instantly aware of his true mission: to show everyone the light. *Cherise was right*, he thought. Things could change.

CHAPTER 10
JULY 25
6:30 P.M.
87°F

Sol wished that she could hail buses on demand. She always seemed to ride the buses on the forgotten routes. Buses with stops without rain covers, lone outposts nervously jutting out of the sidewalk. Buses with schedules that were too complicated to even attempt to fathom: normal stops on Tuesdays, except on streets running northeast to southwest, express stops on Thursdays, except between the hours of some inconvenient time and some other inconvenient time. Buses for brokeasses. Sol actually could afford a cab or a rideshare, but it felt bougie.

Accordingly, Sol stood still as rain continued to deluge her flimsy blue poncho. Cars zoomed by, reaching speeds only intended for highway travel, but she was undisturbed. *Faster traffic means a bus should be here sooner,* she assured herself repeatedly, never convinced.

"Girls are like buses: miss one, next fifteen one coming," she chanted sardonically, wondering what bus Gucci Mane used to catch. Her poncho fluttered around her as the rain continued.

After forty damp minutes, a bus finally arrived, lumbering to the stop. Only one patron was on board, flanking the driver, ready to exit. Sol could already taste the joint she would roll when she finally made it home, inhaling deeply as the bus doors opened, exhaling the sole rider.

Sol climbed the steps, her Breeze Card ready. "Sorry, ma'am," the bus driver said, sticking out a gloved hand in obstruction. "This bus is out of service." Sol shot the woman a look of pure malice then stepped off the bus, the doors whisking shut behind her. A loud decompression followed, the bus slumping over like a beached whale, gases expelling into the air. Why did unavailable buses insist on retiring *in the fucking street*?

Sol felt anger course through her, pooling in her right foot, which she used to kick a half-crushed Coke can into the street. She hated Old National.

The anger left just as quickly as it had come, settling down into disappointment. She had been looking forward to the long, slow bus ride, to the chance to collect herself before the guaranteed stress of dealing with her parents, but rain wasn't relaxing when you were in it. *Traffic it is,* she decided, walking away from the stop and hailing an Uber.

The driver arrived quickly, beckoning her into a white 1991 Cadillac DeVille. Stepping in, Sol marveled at how spacious the back seat was. The driver, a slim

Latino with a sullen face, said little as he sped through the rain, but Sol could feel his eyes flitting toward her.

"Keep your eyes on the fucking road," she warned him.

"Sí, el jefe," the man said sarcastically, suddenly turning on the radio. She understood what he said, but Sol ignored the slight and listened as two excited male broadcasters rifled through the day's news.

"Fulton County Police have linked three separate shootings today to a man in lime-green sneakers. No further details are available at this time, but please contact the police with any tips. Witnesses say the sneakers were unmistakably lime.

"Activists of the political movement Black Lives Matter issued an apology today for tweeting out the wrong address for a flash rally. Fact-checking also matters."

Sol rolled her eyes.

"Polls show that 40 percent of Metro Atlanta residents feel affected by last month's terrorist attack, and 74 percent of Metro Atlanta residents feel another attack is imminent. The investigation of the atrocities is still ongoing. Please contact the FBI with any leads."

"Atrocity? Yeah, right," Sol muttered.

"In other news, charter school Our Children Deserve a Future has won its right to a countywide lottery system, enraging parents who were hoping a win would allow them to enroll their children this upcoming fall. Gwinnett County school officials called the ruling a step toward the fairness all children deserve. The parents who initiated the suit, who all lived within walking distance of the school, called the ruling a tragedy.

"Speaking of tragedies, Andre 3000 of rap group OutKast announced that over two hundred gigabytes of unreleased material were erased from his computer by an overzealous debugging program. A hacker group has offered to help him recover the files. The catch: they only take blank checks."

The driver laughed, annoying Sol. She'd missed the news while she was locked up, but not *this* news, jokes masquerading as concern masquerading as information masquerading as truth masquerading as jokes. She knew everything had a spin, but this kind of news was centrifugal.

An hour later, the rain was still going strong, intensifying as they slid into a still neighborhood off Dekalb Avenue. Sol looked at the humble homes of Melrose Avenue with no nostalgia, watching the sidewalk inexplicably end as they drove deeper into the neighborhood. Sol used to hate having to step off the sidewalk and into the street, looking over her shoulder to avoid speeding vehicles. The only thing she hated more than being watched was having to watch out for the recklessness of others.

"You need me to stay here?" the driver asked, pulling into the driveway of Sol's parents' house. "You never know when the terrorists could strike again."

"No," Sol responded firmly, stepping out of the car. She watched him reverse, walking into the street to ensure he was headed back toward Dekalb. Sol hated when people tried to capitalize off fear. She wasn't above it, but she only did it for survival, not for gain.

Her parents' house was just as she'd left it four years ago, quiet and imposing. Sol struggled to open the door in the rain, eventually realizing the lock had been changed. She huffed, her breath making the hood of her poncho flap up, dampening her hair. She huffed again. The old lock had always been unreliable, jamming every other day, but not being told of the change felt personal. She pressed the doorbell lightly, suddenly hoping no one was home.

Sol's mother appeared, opening the door slowly. Neither of them spoke, long past the stage of veiling their mutual contempt. Sol stared blankly at her mother's half-finished makeup and curlers. She was headed to church. "I thought we would be seeing you soon," her mother finally said, her voice flat.

Sol stepped past her, a perfunctory "Hi, Ma" begrudgingly slipping past clenched teeth. "Where's Pa?" she asked, surveying the foyer.

"He's out back. He made plans to grill without checking the forecast, but I want my grilled steak, so I'm getting my grilled steak." She smiled. Sol ignored it, proceeding to the back patio through the kitchen.

A streak of lightning kept her inside. Instinctively, Sol planted herself in the corner of the kitchen, away from the back door. She removed her soaked poncho and scanned the room. Everything was the same: ragged towels hung sloppily from the refrigerator handle, a loaf of Sara Lee bread sat cozily on top of the microwave, sparkling marble counters. The familiarity was slightly sickening.

Sol's dad burst into the kitchen, the door swinging open and hitting the doorstop on the adjacent wall. Sol had installed the stop after years of her mom pestering her dad about making such rambunctious entrances. It was her first home renovation. Neither of her parents had ever mentioned it.

"The prodigal daughter!" he exclaimed, depositing a tray of steaming steaks onto the counter and approaching Sol with open arms. The steaks smelled delicious, charcoal dashed with smoky rosemary. His police uniform was soaked, but he seemed to be in high spirits.

Sol evaded the attempted hug, placing her hands on his shoulders and locking her elbows, keeping him at arm's length. He should have known better.

As usual, he ignored the obvious distance between them, smiling generously and speaking with casual intimacy. "I am pretty wet, aren't I? So, you're doing pretty all right, I hear?"

"You heard? From who?" Sol said, striding to the other side of the kitchen in one long step.

"Derrick said he saw you last month, said you fixed up Nana's house all nice."

"Is that all he said?"

"Not quite. He also said you own the house now."

"Yep."

"That's a lot of responsibility."

"Sure."

"It is," her mother seconded, stepping into the kitchen draped in a purple Murphy robe, two crosses emblazoned on the sleeves. The curlers were gone, their job finished.

"Revival Week?" Sol asked.

"Of course," her mother replied tersely, retrieving a bowl of salad from the refrigerator.

"I thought so. You always wear your ugliest makeup for Revival."

A familiar silence erupted. Their patience should be running out soon, Sol calculated, excited to have a follow-up to her goading. She had grown out of provocation for provocation's sake. She was now a provocateur with a purpose.

Something was off, though. Her parents had always been masters of the staredown, visible rage administered with invisible techniques, spooky action at a distance. But they seemed oddly relaxed, their faces calm as if they knew something she didn't.

Frustrated, Sol broke the silence. "I'm not selling my fucking house."

"It's not really up to you, dear," her mother assured her.

"What's that supposed to mean?"

"We have evidence that you have been violating your probation. Drugs, alcohol, assault, vandalism," her father stated calmly, using his police officer voice, a throaty drone. Sol had always been annoyed by the fact that he adopted this straightforward tone when he was explaining something arcane. "We've had a PI tailing you for a few weeks," he revealed, opening a drawer and removing a stuffed manila folder. A large photograph peeked out from between its edges. Most of the image was obscured, but Sol saw a cute dog she'd stopped to pet just a week ago. What the hell was happening here?

"What does that have to do with my house?"

He continued. "There's about three thousand dollars' worth of mortgage payments left on the house. You make about thirteen hundred dollars a month. If we give this evidence to your PO, you'll be fined for each violation. This folder contains at least seventy citations. At seventy-five dollars a citation, that's over five thousand dollars, so you're immediately in the hole. If your PO gives this evidence to any of the investigating officers looking into the vandalism cases—which he will—you'll be arrested, which will entail bail, court fees, and probably some fines. Now you're at about seven thousand dollars, and likely some community service. Now, obviously, all of this is theoretically manageable because you don't have to pay these fees upfront. You can pay them over time, but then there's interest. And interest with Georgia, whoo! We have a saying at the precinct: 'You don't want Georgia interested in you.'" He stopped to laugh.

Her mother chimed in. "Long story short, sell us the house for four thousand, and we'll finish off the mortgage and even give you a little windfall."

"You do realize this is extortion, right?" Sol asked, her fists quivering.

"This isn't extortion," Sol's mom responded. "It's a deal. You see, we initially hired the PI just to check on you, make sure you were okay. But based on his reports, you're not okay. You're doing everything that got you into trouble in the first—"

"Instead of asking me if I was okay, you hired someone to spy on me, and then you use that information to bankrupt me?"

"That's not how bankruptcy works, dear. See, you don't even know what you're—"

"I know that you're not taking my fucking house."

"Child, I'm tired of your mouth. Cut me off again, and I will close it. Do you accept the deal or not? I have souls to save and a steak to eat."

Sol stared at the steaks; they were no longer steaming, but their smoky aroma still filled the room. She hadn't felt hungry earlier, but suddenly those steaks were all she could think of.

"Why do you want the house?"

"We need the money," her father replied.

"For what?" Sol asked, her eyes on her dad.

"That's beyond the scope of this transaction," her mother replied.

"No, that's exactly the scope of this conversation. Why am I selling the house of my dead grandmother, that I acquired fair and square, that I signed for at the goddamn bank, that I cleaned up, that I fucking *live in*, to two piece-of-shit parents who don't even have the decency to come to their only daughter's graduation?"

Sol's mother lunged forward, her robes cutting through the air. Her father immediately caught her, grabbing her at the torso and lifting her up. She didn't resist. It reminded Sol of juvie. All that was missing was an unnecessary body slam and someone restraining her as well. Maybe some spit and a "Bitch, you don't want this!" or two for added authenticity.

Sol's mother stood still as she returned to the ground. Her curls were undisturbed, but it was clear that they were on her mind. Her arms were holstered to her sides, pinned, but her eyes kept shooting upward.

Equally tense, Sol surveyed her parents, her dad in his APD uniform, her mom in her church garb. Jerry used to call them "The Law and the Word." Sol had always wondered what that made her.

The standoff continued, rain pouring, steaks cooling, air conditioning humming. Her father's face matched his institutional tone: drab, straightforward, opaque. He'd initially opposed Sol moving in with Nana, his mother, when she started high school, but that opposition had quickly become thick, impenetrable silence.

Thunder shook the house, rattling Sol's mother. *Maybe that's why they haven't kicked me out yet*, Sol realized. Her mom was from the Florida Gulf Coast, the land of storms with names and body counts. Sol used to love when it stormed because that meant her mom would pick her up from school. "You won't need that umbrella," her mom would tell her time and time again, advice she still lived by.

Sol retrieved her poncho from the kitchen counter and headed toward the front door, shaking it as she walked. She reached the door quickly, but hesitated to exit, listening for footsteps or voices. All she heard were shifting plates and clanging utensils.

Outside, the rain continued. Sol considered taking an Uber, but suddenly money seemed tight. Draped in her poncho, she drifted down Melrose, back toward Dekalb, scowling at a street sign that informed her she was on West Howard; she preferred to call it Dekalb. The East Lake MARTA station offered refuge, but she strolled past it, horrified at the thought of returning to a home that might no longer be hers.

Parallel with elevated MARTA tracks, she continued west, her head cloudy, paranoia blooming. Was she really being extorted by a cop and a minister? Somehow that seemed like a more urgent question than why she was being extorted by her parents. She'd heard too many stories in juvie to think that parents were the noble citizens they were supposed to be. Beatings, burnings, pimpings, stabbings, shootings, rapings. Degeneracy and parenthood were far from strangers.

Sol's parents weren't saints, but hiring a PI was a new low, an order of magnitude away from the shouting and strict punishments that she'd been raised on. What in the hell did they need *more* money for? Pa was a captain, and Ma was second-in-command at her church. Their money wasn't good—it was great. Sol felt there was something otherworldly about her situation, something cosmically amiss.

Choked by the humidity, she removed the poncho and slung it over her arm, retreating under an overpass to escape the rain. The ground was wet, so she crouched, her back against a concrete pillar. Raindrops danced around her, paratrooping into puddles and vanishing forever. Sol breathed deeply, the smell of wet crabgrass and red clay filling her nose. Mindlessly, she dug into her pocket and retrieved her phone. She opened the contact list and swiped down and up, names wheeling past like fruits and numbers on a slot machine. She didn't need anyone, she felt. But she wanted someone, a friend.

"Meet me at Variety?" she texted Theo. He texted back quickly, asking for a time. "40 min?" she responded.

"Coo," he said.

Sol rose and put on her poncho. She hated Little Five Points. Too many try-hards and harassers, too many aspiring yuppies and actual yuppies, the worst combination. Of all Atlanta had to offer, why did people persist on frequenting this nub of a neighborhood?

She hated concerts in Little Five Points even more. Because it was one of the few places in town that featured good acts for good prices, she had to go. Things normally went well, but on those few occasions she'd seized an ass-grabbing hand and twisted back its desperate fingers, *she* had been the one who was restrained and thrown out. Still, for her purposes, it worked. The beauty of the Variety Playhouse and Little Five Points in general was that you always knew who was supposed to be there and who wasn't. Tourists—in all forms, whether they were visiting a new place, a new scene, or a new version of themselves—were always visible. If she really were being tailed by a PI, this would be the place to find out. Sol just hoped she wasn't the tourist. Variety lived up to its name, so this could easily turn out poorly. She stepped out into the rain, headed toward Mclendon.

Theo was outside when she arrived, packed among a mob huddling under Variety's small rain cover. On sight, Sol laughed at his inexplicable hoodie. He really didn't get it.

Theo greeted her with a hug and a smile, quickly stepping back to wipe his forehead. Sol wasn't sure if it was sweat or rain.

"Are we really about to see a Mystikal cover band?" Theo asked, scanning the bill. "I know we haven't hung out in a while, but this is pretty weird."

Sol grimaced; she hadn't even liked regular Mystikal.

"No, let's just get something to eat," she said, stepping back out into the rain, the ridiculousness of her plan settling in. A PI could be anybody, anywhere at any time. She wasn't going to catch anyone spying, especially a professional. If she wanted to get her parents off her ass, she'd have to get personal. Zed, Apollo, and Kai had vetoed her request to tag Derrick's houses. Obviously, they'd have to change their minds.

"So, what's up with you?" Theo asked as they slid into opposite sides of a booth in a smoke-filled restaurant. "You've been pretty quiet since we left Variety."

Sol stared at her menu, recalling fragments of her last trip to the Vortex. She had ordered a burger of some sort, but it had been a burger in the most generic sense. It had all the burger elements—meat, salt, cheese, bread—but not any lasting bonds between them. She'd dressed it carefully, placing the lettuce, tomato, onion, and Texas Pete in perfect harmony, but defense didn't win games.

Before she could answer Theo, the waiter, a white woman with a tattoo of Wyoming on her forearm and burgundy lipstick smothered over thin lips, appeared and asked for her order. Sol hated when people didn't know what they were ordering, so she ordered the same thing she had last time. Theo didn't seem fazed by being rushed. Good.

"Not much," Sol finally answered. Theo shrugged and eagerly chatted away, asking about everyone and everything except Kai. Sol didn't fill him in. There wasn't much to say.

Their food came quickly. The waiter informed them that she'd told the cooks to give them priority. "I like the way you look," she'd answered when Sol asked why. Sol watched the slow shuffle of her hips as she walked away. She didn't trust her.

"What's wrong with you?" Theo asked as he prepared his burger, drenching it in hot sauce.

Sol glared at her meal. An oversized burger embedded in a sea of fries glared back at her. There was something pathetic about how stylish the burger looked: toasted brioche bun, crisp romaine lettuce, fresh mozzarella, heirloom tomatoes. It was supposed to be a goddamn burger, not a pageant contestant.

"I've been dealing with some stuff, heavy stuff." She paused. "But you know what? I'm good. I'm like, really good," she declared, exiting the booth. "In fact, fuck this place and their mediocre, overpriced, overrated burgers. I want a fucking steak."

"These prices really aren't that bad," Theo muttered, removing his wallet.

Sol groaned as he lingered to count out the money for their deserted meal. Theo never missed a chance to do the right thing. It was so annoying.

Outside, the rain continued, pattering softly on the trash-strewn sidewalk. Sol held her breath as she stepped over an army of roaches that was thorax-deep in a pile of discarded french fries. "Roaches are the worst," she said, exhaling and pointing at the repulsive orgy of potatoes and chitin.

"Those are actually water bugs," Theo said. Sol grimaced into a smile. That was something Nana would say.

They stopped at the intersection of McClendon and Moreland. Sol had never ordered a steak in a restaurant before. She wasn't even sure where steaks were sold. Clueless, she pulled out her phone and searched "steakhouse." The nearest and most highly rated result was Kevin Rathbun Steak, off of Krog. She hated Krog Street. Before juvie, she had made it her life's mission to slash every wholesome mural on the street. But she'd since given up and ceded her mission to Zed. Those Living Walls murals never seemed to die.

"Where are you parked?" she asked Theo, who was facedown in his phone.

"Right across from Variety," he replied.

"Cool, I found a place."

He nodded and pocketed his phone. Sol knew calling Theo was the right choice. He never asked questions.

The drive was brief, maybe not even five full minutes. They parked in an empty lot and stepped back into the rain, which had slowed to a trickle. A repurposed warehouse stood before them, worn brick and high ceilings, a fort of a building, squat and sturdy. Theo reached the door first, stepping to the side to open it for Sol. "Such a charmer," Sol joked, bowing before stepping inside.

Dim lights, black metal, and rustic wood greeted them, followed by the host, a coiffed young white man. "Table for two?" he queried.

Sol nodded.

"Do you have a reservation?"

"No."

"Hmm. That might be a problem."

"How so?"

"We're pretty full tonight. The wait could be up to three hours."

"This is full?" Sol asked, motioning toward a section full of empty seats.

"Yes," the host answered, his voice apologetic.

"This doesn't look full to me."

"Unfortunately, what you see doesn't tell the whole story," the host said, pointing at his iPad and smiling.

Sol stared at him, her eyes fixed on his crabby faux smile. He was beyond words.

Sol removed her poncho and thoroughly shook it out, the plastic cutting through the air and slinging water over the host, his podium, his iPad, the fresh mints, and even herself. The host remained silent throughout, his body as stiff as his coiffure. But Sol knew he had got the message.

"Are you sure you can't squeeze us in? Technology gets things wrong sometimes, right?"

The host swiped through the iPad like a frenzied maestro then grabbed two menus and led them to a table adjoining a wall.

"Thank you so much," Sol exclaimed as he departed to his podium.

"You know they're going to put, like, AIDS in our meal, right?" Theo informed her as he unfolded his cloth napkin.

"Probably. But that would still be better than anything I ate in juvie."

They laughed then peeled open their menus, two bound and embroidered booklets the size of a folded newspaper. The waiter came soon after, taking their orders and reclaiming their menus. Sol was sad to see them go. Even after she had decided what she would eat, she was fascinated by the odd combinations dashed throughout the menu: parsnips and peppercorns, pecans and parsley.

They sat in silence, taking in the scene. Waiters shuffling from table to table, busboys boomeranging from the kitchen, the bartender bounding up and down the bar, hands always full, with either money or beverages. Sol could have enjoyed that silence forever, but she knew Theo was going to break.

"So, what's with you and steak?" he asked in a joking yet serious tone.

"Just wanted to step it up, treat myself a little."

"I feel that. I've actually been keeping it low-key lately. Cutting grass, trying to save money to fix my car."

"Yeah? Sorry about that."

"No worries. You took control of things."

"Somebody had to. You really fucked up."

"I know, I know. The guy seemed legit, though."

"No one on Craigslist is legit."

"I don't know. A few weeks ago, I picked up some books through Craigslist. They were pretty legit."

"Yeah? What'd you pull?"

"It was a crazy haul. Some older lady out in Villa Rica—used to be a professor—was giving all her books away so she could move to California. Apparently, she hates both Amazon and her local library, and Goodwill, and Salvation Army—actually, I think they hate her, wasn't clear. She refused to just leave the books on the street, so she was posting on the internet and hitting up the local McDonald's and the QuikTrip and even the fucking car wash. She was determined."

"That's crazy."

"Yeah, I picked up some music books and some Walter Mosley stuff and some comics, and Apollo picked up an original printing of the autobio of Malcolm X. Remember when Coach Greene made us read that?"

"Sure do. Best book I've ever read. I read it twice in juvie."

"I don't know about 'best book,' but that's cool. You should talk to Apollo about it. He's been reading it a lot lately."

"What are his thoughts? As usual, I'm sure he has a bunch."

Theo paused. "I don't know, honestly. I feel like I understand that book pretty well, but Apollo is on some other shit."

"What do you mean?"

"He's just been saying stuff about how Malcolm was brave to turn his back on the Nation of Islam and how we should all know when we have to advance the discourse. Weird shit like that."

"He's kind of right, but that's only one part of the book. It's really about how in life, Malcolm comes to realize that being part of a movement or an organization shouldn't mean becoming, like, a puppet. Malcolm turned his back on the Nation not because he was some forward thinker, but because he realized the world was bigger and that Islam itself was bigger than the Nation allowed it to be. And he didn't really even turn his back on them. He stepped away for the sake of his own beliefs and growth."

"Oh shit, young scholar on deck," Theo announced, tapping his fork on an empty wine glass.

"I know a thing or two," Sol said.

Silence descended again, this time more resolute, comfortable. Sol wondered whether strong-arming the host counted as a violation of her probation. She probably didn't want to know the answer, she realized, settling back into silence.

The food arrived unceremoniously, the waitstaff wordlessly sliding plates onto the table, metal and porcelain somehow mute despite dangerous proximity. *Why was fine dining so damn quiet?* Sol wondered, thinking of the unending noise of her own shift: that blaring jukebox, that rusty bathroom door, those squeaky, incessantly mopped floors.

Patiently, she carved her steak into bite-size chunks, amazed at how effortlessly the browned flesh parted as the knife advanced through it, a Red Sea of tenderness. This was that upper echelon shit.

She coated the morsel in a film of mashed potatoes and took her first bite. The taste was exactly all right. She took a bite without the mashed potatoes. Still just all right, maybe slightly worse. By her fourth bite, she was exchanging grins with Theo, who was also unimpressed.

"Well, you got your steak," he sighed.

"Yeah, I guess I did," Sol said.

CHAPTER 11
JULY 28
6:12 P.M.
90°F

TILLY KNEW EXACTLY WHAT TO EXPECT WHEN A subjectless email containing a YouTube link streaked across her phone. It damn sure wasn't the latest *Jimmy Fallon* clip. Halting right in the middle of the Kroger, her basket unfilled, Tilly watched the video, sighing.

"The destruction of a racist monument is a beautiful thing, but instead of talking about free speech and terrorism, how about we discuss the union of surveillance and weaponry? How about we talk about a weapon that can destroy entire neighborhoods? How about we talk about how looking up at the sky is now like looking down the barrel of a police gun?"

Goddamn, she's good, Tilly thought, admiring the impassioned activist, a young black woman, debating in the video. Too bad she represented Black Lives Matter. Quantico had been investigating them for some time. "Black identity extremists," they were called internally, whatever the fuck that meant. In reality, they were just regular Americans with justified grievances. But once you were on that watch list, you stayed there until you were useful.

The debate continued, but Tilly stopped watching it, plugging in her headphones and beginning to fill her basket. She'd seen all she needed to see. #FireAndBrimStoneMountain was a trending topic again, and Black Lives Matter had brought it back to life. Meddling fucking kids. Why were activists so damn impatient? The deluge of press emails had just slowed to a trickle a few weeks ago, finally allowing her to do her actual job—following leads and profiling perps—instead of doing PR.

Tilly longed for her days as a junior agent, when work ended as soon as she shut down her office computer and life began as soon as she started her home computer. Rick called them her "Lisbeth" days, after Lisbeth Salander of *Dragon Tattoo* fame, but Tilly knew better. She'd hacked for the personal challenge, the thrill of expanding her skills. She didn't have any political goal or business interest or vengeance to claim. Hacking, for her, was like running on a treadmill: pure artifice, no ambition, no destination, no stakes.

Those days of hacking all night were long gone, along with her patience and her body's ability to process copious amounts of Mountain Dew. After speeding through the beverage aisle, she hurried to the checkout lane, eager to get back to the office. Every second counted if she wanted to keep her boss, Fitz Houndum, off her ass.

"I knew you had a secret mini fridge!" Rick exclaimed as Tilly barged into her office, grocery bags in tow. She knew she was on the losing end when she agreed to exchange office keys with him, yet she'd still agreed to do it. "Partners must be equal," he'd argued.

"I never denied it," Tilly replied, placing her bags in the fridge in her closet. *Rick better not have a key to this, too,* she thought as she closed and locked the closet door. Exhausted, she collapsed into her office chair, taking a deep breath.

"I have no idea how to handle the Black Lives Matter stuff. I know it will blow over, but I don't know if this case can wait that long. Everything is cold, and we have no prime suspect, no motive, no leads. And Mr. Mystery Government Guy keeps blowing off Houndum."

Rick grinned back her, relishing her anguish. "Actually, we've got one out of four," he said after a spell.

"Are those our chances of being demoted?" Tilly asked.

"No. I just got a tip that blew this case all the way the fuck open. Apparently, the van that got wrecked was sold to our mysterious terrorists that same night. And check this: the terrorists were teenagers."

"No fucking way. So, this is domestic?" Tilly perked up, leaning across her desk, a gesture typically reserved for realizing the building was closing.

"This is very domestic. The guy who sold the van says he sold it to some young black kid in a blue Honda Civic."

Tilly was instantly skeptical. "A young black kid? That's weird. I mean, I guess that fits the nature of the crime, but even then, I don't see it. What black teen in 2019 has strong opinions on Civil War memorials?" Tilly paused, concentrating. Leads were like relationships. If you didn't recognize where they were taking you early on, you could waste a lot of good time. And outfits.

"I'm not sure this is domestic, Rick," Tilly declared. "He could have been African. Or Caribbean. Or Canadian. Before we get to that, though, can we trust this source of yours? Who is he? What does he do? How did he meet the kid? Why did he come in?"

"I don't know all that shit, Tilly. You're the *actual* senior agent. I'm just a specialist who got a title change because human resources doesn't know what they're doing. He's in Interrogation Room F, though, if you want to interview him."

Grabbing a clipboard and a tablet, Tilly bolted out of her office, marching toward the interrogation rooms. Rick tailed her, straining to keep up, his worn sneakers squeaking loudly through the still and empty halls.

Quietly, they entered the antechamber of the interrogation room, standing on the opaque side of the room's one-way mirror, watching their tipper sweat onto the room's wide table. Tilly immediately recognized him.

"I think he walked here," Rick speculated. "He smelled like Buford Highway, if you know what I mean."

"I don't know what you mean, and I encourage you not to clarify."

They continued to look through the mirror, watching the tipper continue to sweat. He wore plain clothing—jeans and an imageless black T-shirt—but he had a strange pride about him. His hair was immaculately wavy, his hairline delicately sculpted, and his cropped sideburns jutted down his face, terminating in a crisp needle point. He had no jewelry, but his skin shone like it had been rinsed in sunlight. He was trying to keep a low profile, "trying" being the operative word.

Tilly smiled, happy at her fortune. "Anything else I need to know before I question this guy?"

"According to the forms we had him fill out, his name is George Curio. The basics are that he lives in East Point off of Newnan Street, he was born in 1983 in Coweta County, he's American, unmarried, and works as an entrepreneur. My guess is that he's a pimp, but I just associate waves with pimping. Not sure why. I could never get waves. My friends said I always had the wrong brush, but I think that was their way of keeping my hope alive."

Tilly scowled. Rick never knew when to shut it off. "Thanks, Rick. I'll take care of this interview. You go look up his online profile and search our databases for any criminal history. Use his address, but don't search for George Curio. It sounds a little too much like Curious George to me. Look up outstanding cases of car theft and cross-reference that with armed robbery."

Satisfied, she paused then added, "I think you might find something interesting."

Rick nodded before waltzing out of the room, leaving Tilly alone. Rick had missed her hints. Their partnership needed work. Or at least a few more Magic City visits.

Keeping her eye on George, Tilly reviewed the case details, preparing her interview questions. It had taken her years, but she'd finally learned to stop treating interviews as open-ended. There were benefits to allowing the interviewee to get comfortable, to gradually drop their defense and answer honestly. But you only got glimpses when you watched someone voluntarily disarm. If you wanted an unobstructed view of the fiber of their fabric, you had to confront them in full armor, scanning for the chinks that were guarded most carefully. "A point guard that never shoots probably has a bad shot," Tilly's high school basketball coach used to say.

George dribbled his fingers on the table as Tilly walked into the room. "About fucking time. I come here to do my city a favor, and you act like you're doing me a favor, strolling in all casual and shit with your damn blond highlights and modern pantsuit. Bitch, you ain't Keri Hilson."

Tilly seated herself without responding. Voluntary leads always overvalued themselves, lashing out so they could glean their actual value. If they were immediately scolded, they knew they had overshot it and quickly simmered down; if they were received warmly, they knew they had guessed just right and began to state their terms. They never accounted for indifference, though. Tilly scribbled out her questions as George stared at her, bewildered, sweat visibly pooling in the folds of his neck and continuing to drip onto the table.

After completing her list of questions, Tilly clicked her pen shut and observed George directly, remaining silent. He avoided her gaze, his eyes limply falling to the table.

"I didn't do shit. I swear," he eventually stuttered out. "I met the kid on Craigslist in May. Never met him before that. I promised him a van I had boosted, and on the night in question, I met up with him and sold it to him in person, cash. That's it. See how honest I'm being? I admit that I boosted the van." Tilly stared back at him.

"Are you even listening to me? You come in here scribbling shit, but I'm giving you everything you need to know, and your pen is lying on the table like a fucking paperweight. Are you an agent or a fucking secretary?"

Tilly jerked forward, lunging at George from across the table like an outfielder fetching a fly ball. She seized George's lumpy neck, grasping it tightly, his milky sweat coating her palms. "What do you think?" she responded, watching the color evaporate from his face. His hands desperately slithered around her taut forearm, pleading for mercy.

Tilly squeezed tighter, his pulse resounding through her wrists like a frenzied drumbeat. His hands moved more wildly, his dull fingernails scrabbling to break her skin, her concentration, anything.

Tilly held tight, invigorated by her anger. There was a palpable pleasure in his raw desperation, his supplicating eyes. She gripped tighter.

George began to squirm, his body jerky and wild. Satisfied, Tilly finally relented, flinging George away and settling back into her chair as he collapsed onto his knees, sputtering out garbled breaths. Eventually, he slowly rose, staggering his way up his chair legs and plopping into the seat. Tilly could feel his pulse from across the room. Clicking on the recorder embedded into the table, she began the official interrogation.

"Hi, Mr. Curio, I am Tilly Erickson, Senior Agent, Cybercrimes Division. You are here today, July 28, to discuss potentially important information regarding the recent terrorist strikes on Stone Mountain. Your compliance is completely voluntary, and no charges have been brought against you at this time. However, you are strongly encouraged to answer openly and clearly about your involvement in this incident. There is nothing preventing you from becoming a suspect. Am I clear?"

George nodded, his bloodshot eyes anchored to the floor.

"Mr. Curio, please respond verbally, for the record," Tilly instructed, a smile tugging at her lips.

"Yes," he coughed out, his voice scratching through the air.

"Great, now we can begin," Tilly announced, clicking her pen and twirling it in her fingers. "What is your occupation, Mr. Curio?"

"I'm a used car salesman. I buy and sell used cars."

"How long have you been a used car salesman?"

"About five years."

"Where do you get your cars?"

"Just here and there, you know."

"I don't. That's why I asked."

"Um, mostly clunkers on Craigslist and estate sales out in the boondocks."

"Where do you store your cars?"

"Next question."

"Where do you store your cars?"

"That's proprietary information. It can't be recorded."

Tilly leaned forward and clicked off the recorder. George eyed her closely. A small thump came from behind her. Someone was leaning on the mirror. They were being watched. Curio stared at the mirror.

"Are you ready to answer my question, Mr. Curio?" Tilly inquired.

"Are you ready to suck my dick?"

Tilly suppressed a chuckle. He really thought that she'd choked him because she'd lost her cool, because she had a temper like some down-and-out *Law & Order* cop dealing with a divorce and the death of a partner. What a fool. Tilly didn't have a temper. She'd choked his monkey ass because she had authority. Nothing further was needed. She decided to toss out a lifeline.

"Mr. Curio, I don't have time for games. I know you think you have a friend on the other side of the mirror, but you don't. The person watching this interview is my boss. Notice how he didn't burst into the room a few minutes ago? That's because you don't mean shit to him. So, let's get to the point. I know that you sell crappy weed out of your grandmother's house in East Point. I know that there are warrants for your arrest in Gwinnett County, Fulton County, and Coweta County. I know that you find cars for sale on Craigslist then stick up their owners and go back to Craigslist to sell those cars. We've actually been monitoring you for a few months, so I'm quite familiar with who you are, Eric Sims. Did you really think that your idiotic hustle was going unwatched? You've been stealing Benzes and Lexuses in a city where people spend more money on their cars than their educations."

He stared back at her, his eyes suddenly alert. Tilly continued.

"You were doing fine with Camrys—we bought a few from you—but you just had to level up. Well, this is the next level. You can stay here with me, in an FBI interrogation room, face-to-face with the lead investigator on your stupid, worthless case, or you can answer my questions, never see me again, and steal as many shitty Camrys as you want. The choice is yours, Eric." Tilly clicked on the recorder, easing back into her chair and looking forward to loosening her taut ponytail when she got back to her office.

Sims glared at her, malice overtaking his manicured face, his facade melting away. Tilly pointed at the recorder, and Sims sighed, his resignation drifting through the cramped room.

"The kid pulled up in a blue Civic, an old model, like '98 or '99. The car had two broads in it. One had mad red hair. Like Rihanna red, you know what I mean?"

Tilly nodded.

"The other looked kind of rough, like she would beat a bitch with a bottle, not because a bottle was nearby, but because she carried a bottle for beating bitches. She was dark-skinned. There was a MINI parked in front of the Civic. It was black."

"What states were the license plates from?"

"You really lucked out, huh? Fucking with a car thief."

Tilly's arms flung into the air, gesticulating wildly at the recorder. Five months monitoring this fool and she still hadn't fathomed the depth of his idiocy.

"I mean, they looked like car thieves, you know. Very fast and furious. Very, uh, multicultural? But anyway, they were both from Georgia. The MINI was from Clayton, and the Civic was from Cobb. They were probably stolen, though, so I don't know if that means anything." Thrilled to have finally caught on, he winked.

Tilly continued. "How old were they? Where were they from, you'd say?"

"I don't know where they were from. They were bumping Gucci when they pulled up, but Gucci is global these days, so I don't know. The kid had kind of an accent, but he could have just went to private school. He was American, though, if that's what you're asking. Speaking of school, I'd say he was still in it. He had no facial hair, and he had those baby waves. You could tell he hadn't had to work for them."

"How had you corresponded with him? Phone? Internet?"

"Both. Most of my clients pick one and stick to it, but he emailed me and called me. He was very suspicious."

"Do you still have his contact information on your computer?"

"Computer? Bitch, I'm modern. I do all my business through my phone. But yeah, I keep all of my clients' records. I gave my phone to the guy who signed me in. I hope it will help, but he probably had a burner. Those car thieves, I hear they like those. I think I saw that in a VICE documentary." He winked again.

"Were the perps armed?"

"How the hell would I know? I didn't pat them down. I just sold them a fucking vehicle." Tilly rose from her seat. Sims was well past being useful. Before she could click off the recorder, he added, "But based on what I've seen in my *experiences*, they weren't intimidating, you know? I'm no criminal profiler or anything because I'm just a businessman, but they seemed super focused, like they had a mission. If I was rolling five deep and I was a criminal, I probably would have just taken the van, but they paid me for it."

"How much?" Tilly asked.

"A thousand. But I gave them three hundred back. The brakes weren't so good. I wanted them to be safe. Dead clients don't come back, you know?"

"Thank you very much, Mr. Curio. I will be in contact if I need anything else from you."

Tilly clicked off the recorder and exited the room. Houndum was gone. He'd probably left after he'd realized she was nowhere near resolving the Black Lives Matter development. Whatever, that wasn't her job. She hoped he had caught the choking before he left. "You know we're not cops, right?" he had asked her after supervising her first suspect interview when she moved to the Atlanta office. She didn't know what he meant then, but she'd learned. Cops were defined by their authority. That's why they wigged out when they lost it or it was questioned. Tilly had scoffed when she saw her coworkers supporting #BlueLivesMatter on Facebook. Cops were so fucking needy.

Agents were defined by their resources, authority being just one among many others. Agents didn't have to restrain themselves because of a code or pretend to be ashamed when they transgressed that code. There was no good agent/bad agent routine. There was just investigation. And good investigators closed their cases by using all of the resources at their disposal, choking included.

Case details swirled in her head as Tilly made her way back to her office. Sims had given her silhouettes, but at least things were no longer shapeless. She still couldn't figure out why African American teenagers would be hijacking a government satellite, but if they had the money and the know-how to pull it off, they had to mostly have been from Cobb. The Clayton county tag would have to be looked into, but Clayton County barely produced graduates; there was no way it was producing terrorists.

"You look content," Rick said as she entered her office.

"You look comfortable," Tilly replied, eyeing his outstretched legs, which were resting on her bookshelf.

"I am. The case is back on track! I watched the live feed of the interview. I can't believe the recorder routine still works. These plebeians really think that the FBI records interviews using a tape recorder that is embedded in a table. We always leave them in the room alone for at least fifteen minutes, phones confiscated, and they still never seem to notice the damn closed-circuit camera in the corner. I think *CSI: Miami* might have permanently ruined criminality. It's really a shame because we depend on the criminals to do our jobs well."

"Are you finished?"

"Yeah, I got Sims's phone from the front desk. I'm going to call up AT&T and request the logs first thing tomorrow."

"Good. Anything else?"

"Sims was probably right about them using burners. But maybe Saint Snowden will bless us, and we'll score some actual recorded calls. Knowing the perps' voices won't help us find out who they are if we don't already have voiceprints, but it will help us verify once we know."

"Do you feel like we're closer to knowing?" Tilly asked, needing him to answer confidently.

"Slightly. We've got car models and counties. We can try to pull some surveillance footage from the night. Both Cobb and Clayton are off the interstate, so maybe we'll get something. That new car recognition software from ATF can recognize car colors and models pretty well, but it will still be a lot of images, so we will have to choose very accurate parameters. Plus, now that we know this is 'just' a domestic case, that NSA money is probably gonna get cut off, so no awesome supercomputers to do all the work. We'll have to use our eyeballs!"

That was slightly reassuring, Tilly thought. "Maybe, maybe not," she offered. "Houndum saw the interview himself, so he knows this is domestic, but if we connect it to this Black Lives Matter stuff, he can convince the higher-ups to let us keep access to the computers for a few more weeks. They've got connections with Palestinian activists. It's nothing substantial, but for our audience, that doesn't matter."

"Finally sounding like a closer. I see you!" Rick said as he dropped his legs to the floor and sprung from his seat. He left quietly, gathering his gear and exiting with a quick wave.

Tilly remained standing, slowly pacing her office. Rick hadn't mentioned that the lead suspect of one of their cases had just come and become the lead witness for another case. How had that not come up?

Maybe it was pride. He had processed Sims and hadn't recognized him. Or at least he hadn't shown recognition. Tilly wasn't sure why she hadn't flat-out told him about Sims instead of dropping hints. Maybe she was testing the waters. Eccentric personality aside, Rick had always been a great partner. They had closed every case they'd worked on together, with minimal need for overtime. And Rick had never been off his game. But he still needed to earn his keep, and missing alley-oops wasn't acceptable. He hadn't even mentioned the fact that they let Sims go. Weird.

Tilly contemplated the Sims case. They'd been assigned to Sims after he'd jacked an old Lexus from an Atlanta councilwoman's son. He should have been brought in by Atlanta's finest, but Houndum finessed his way into getting the investigation picked up by the FBI and insisted that they build a huge case against him. "Free publicity," he'd written in the subject line of the email assigning the case. #FireandBrimStoneMountain was certainly better publicity, and thus a better promotion, but it wasn't like Rick to leave a case open or to make mistakes, even for a better case. *He must be really stressed,* Tilly concluded.

She sat down at her desk and studied her face in her pocket mirror. She was definitely stressed, but she looked better than she'd expected. *Black don't crack, but it damn sure stretches,* she thought, chuckling to herself. The sight of her smile made her pause. She hadn't seen it in a while; it was almost unfamiliar.

Ready for sleep, Tilly retrieved her groceries and headed for her car, dwelling on the odd surprise of having forgotten what she looked like when she smiled. As she drove home, she wondered how it would feel to completely forget, her mind electrified by the possibility.

CHAPTER 12
JULY 31
10:37 P.M.
87°F

Tilly was lost after three turns. The Georgia Cybersecurity Command Center was a simple building—clear sight lines, long corridors, large, sun-seeking windows—but it had the soul of a labyrinth. Its every element encouraged paranoia. The walls were blindingly white, the artwork was unmemorable, the rooms weren't numbered, the people ducked their heads. It was as if the entire building was one continuous surface, expanding in all directions yet leading nowhere, an architectural koan. Rick's tacky Nikes, a schlocky, ectoplasmic green, were the only object in her field of vision that had definite shape, but even they were becoming an indistinct blur as their escort—he hadn't told them his name—led them deeper into the atrium of the complex.

After more turns and two card swipes, they eventually turned into an unremarkable room filled with overflowing binders stuffed onto dusty metal shelves. None of the binders were labeled, but nothing seemed out of place. The room had the clutter of a janitor's closet and the organization of an evidence locker. Tilly and Rick watched silently as their escort sifted through the stacks and then removed five heavy binders, struggling to transfer them to a nearby desk. "No," he barked when Rick attempted to help him with the load. "You can only access these documents through me, and that includes touching them."

"I hope that doesn't mean we'll be holding hands," Rick joked. The escort didn't laugh.

"Why all the secrecy?" Tilly asked.

Both the escort and Rick glared at her. *Because it's the NSA, dummy,* she answered flatly in her head.

"Because most Americans don't like the idea of their government keeping files on teenagers," the escort said. "But most Americans don't know what some teenagers are up to, so managing that disconnect is up to us. And I mean us, not the CIA, or the DoD, or the press, or the FBI. No offense."

Tilly sighed as quietly as she could. "So, now that we're in this room," Rick said, "'we' as in my partner and I, and you, no offense, what can you tell us? And why the fuck do you still keep paper files?"

"We keep paper files because Russia doesn't tend to hack into doors. And I can tell you about five possible perps who we have been following in the Atlanta region who might have committed the attack you're investigating." Stiffly, he began opening the binders and spreading their contents over the desk. A sea of photographs and printed computer screenshots quickly drifted across the desk. Tilly wasn't sure where to begin.

The escort took the lead. "So, these two fit the standard profile for teen cybercrime in Georgia," he began, gesturing at two printed portraits, both featuring names in bold print in the white space: Trevor Jenkins and Kurt Peters. "White, male, Libertarian, agnostic, decent grades. Forgettable in the real world, but menaces online. It's mostly petty stuff. Spamming teachers they don't like, distributing nude photographs of former girlfriends. Basically trolling gone a little too far. Good kids who need some guidance. "This one"—he jabbed his finger onto the asymmetrical nose of Trevor Jenkins—"could probably go to MIT if he just applied himself. Perfect SAT scores. He'll probably just end up at GT, though."

"I think you're taking this Big Brother thing too literally," Rick replied. Tilly kept her eyes on the escort's finger, afraid to meet Rick's conspiring eyes and erupt into laughter.

"So, are they our perps?" Tilly asked, still looking down.

"Probably not," the escort stammered. "Like I said, these two are trolls. Everything they do is to stoke a specific reaction, namely, laughter among other white males. They don't have any discernible political agenda, and they live in Augusta."

"Then why are you telling us about them?" Rick asked.

The escort smiled, something Tilly hadn't thought he was capable of. "Because this whole situation is pretty funny, if you ask me."

"How so?" Tilly asked. She could already see a conspiratorial grin gliding across Rick's face. Nothing brought black men together like shared contempt for their jobs.

"No offense, but who the fuck cares about Stone Mountain? It's a theme park on the outskirts of Atlanta that got one shout-out in the 'I Had a Dream' speech. It has the largest bas-relief in the world, but only ten people in the world even know what a damn bas-relief is. Sure, the Klan has the occasional rally there, but politically, it's dead. People go there to picnic and walk and have fitness boot camps so they can fit into their bridesmaid dresses. Stone Mountain Park could be any park."

Tilly glanced at Rick. His grin had vanished entirely, replaced by the serenity of mutual recognition. *I'm not the only one,* Tilly knew him to be thinking. The only time she'd seen him look that at ease was when she'd mentioned that she'd once had a summer internship at a small record label in DC. He'd responded with that same look, right before badgering her for two hours, then months, about her experience. He'd had an internship at an Atlanta label, So So Def, she'd learned, along with his favorite So So Def song ("Just Kickin' It"), his favorite music video ("Lean wit It, Rock wit It"), his favorite album cover (*The Movement*), and a dozen other extraneous facts. She wasn't venturing down that road again. Bulk data—on anyone—was for the NSA. The FBI gathered evidence.

"Thanks for the analysis, but we're just here for perps. Who are these other three?" She glared at Rick. *Don't even fucking think about it,* she signaled with that special scowl she usually reserved for street harassers and perps who refused to be arrested by a woman. He nodded.

"These other three are a bit more unique," the escort began, brushing aside the portraits of Jenkins and Peters. "The first thing you'll probably notice is that they're African American, which is unusual among cybercriminals in Georgia. I stick by my analysis, but I will admit that there are some odd behaviors among these three."

"First…" He picked up two portraits, waving them loosely. "We've been watching these two, but we've never actually caught them doing any illegal activity. Our monitoring campaign has been very thorough, including access to their phones, email accounts, and social media, as well as field agents occasionally tailing them, but we've yet to confirm their involvement in anything of concern."

"So why are you telling us about them?" Tilly asked.

"Because I think they're hiding something. Apollo Aleyani, especially. There's no reason a seventeen-year-old in Clayton County should be using VPNs, end-to-end encrypted messaging, and IP scramblers. It raises all kinds of alarms."

"Sure," Tilly said. "What else can you tell me about them?"

"They are both affiliated with a known graffiti gang, and Theo Santos is quite fond of rap music."

"Criminal records?" Rick asked.

"No."

"Misdemeanors? School suspensions?" Tilly asked.

"Nope."

"Bad grades?" Tilly and Rick inquired in unison.

"Honor—"

"—I think we've heard enough, next," Rick interrupted.

Tilly swallowed a laugh and nodded. "Well, this last one hasn't been monitored as closely, but she's been on our radar for about seven years," the escort said.

"Seven years?" Tilly scoffed. "But she's only seventeen."

"When she was ten, she used a laptop to delete a federal employee's dental plan."

"Are you serious?" Rick asked. Tilly could sense him winding up for a punchline.

"Entirely. It was a mistake, we were told, but it was technically tampering with government records, so we've been keeping tabs on her just in case she was actually an agent provocateur. Kids are rarely what we think they are. Believe me, I manage her file. You'd be surprised at what she's capable of."

"I bet she throws a mean hackathon," Rick sneered.

"So far, we've found no evidence that she hacks recreationally, but—"

"Thank you for your time," Tilly announced, turning toward the door. The hallway and the building at large were just as authoritarian as they had been before, but somehow, she knew her way out, easily making it back to the lobby, the escort shuffling behind her. She'd always thought the labyrinth was the Minotaur's home, but maybe it was his prison.

"Why don't these NSA guys ever tell us their names," Rick commented as they crossed the parking lot, the Command Center looming behind them.

"The same reason strippers never give you their phone numbers."

Rick immediately brandished his phone. "I got fifty digits and three photo albums that will make you eat, digest, and shit those words. But I'll play ball. Hit me."

"Because you're supposed to leave your phone in the car, but you never do."

o o o

Tilly tensed when she saw Rick swivel the audio knob to the left. He turned down his music for two reasons and two reasons only: when he had a hopeless business plan, or when he had a breakthrough. Tilly hoped, prayed, and pleaded for the latter.

"You know," he began, "I know this trip was unproductive, but he did mention Clayton County, and Santos was from Cobb. I'm inclined to follow up on both."

"You can't be serious," Tilly said. "That intel was garbage. Did you hear how smug he sounded? 'It raises all kinds of alarms.' All he had were suspicions—no evidence, no analysis, no casing. Absolutely amateur. This is why no one trusts them. They look through your windows just because you have curtains. Who knows why kids do what they do? You want me to bring the force of the state down upon two teens just because some analysts can't tell secrecy from security? Fuck that. Rick, this is the difference between us and them. We build cases from working, not guessing. You think I'm going to put my name behind a nothing case like that? I only use this word when I'm mad, so don't you ever bring this up again, but nigga, you're out your goddamn mind."

Rick paused before speaking, a rare move. "It doesn't matter if the intel is garbage. I'm not saying we move based on what his shit analysis can do for the case. I'm saying we move based on what that intel can do for us. This is like a free life. They gathered all these dots. We just have to connect them. If they're wrong, so be it. But if they're not, we save time and effort, and we get all the credit. I know you like the hunt, but why search for new prey when we already have game in our net? Think about it."

Tilly flicked down an AC vent and reclined her seat, gazing out onto Piedmont Avenue. The music resumed.

"And they wonder why niggas get shot," pondered Vince Staples.

AUGUST

AVERAGE HIGH: 93°F

AVERAGE LOW: 74°F

CHAPTER 13
AUGUST 4
2:12 P.M.
98°F

Inertia crept up Apollo's body with a surprising grace. The garage door was opening at 2:12 p.m. on a weekday, and he had not just one but three members of the opposite sex seated at his dining room table. The bike in the driveway could be lied away; the girls weren't as easily dismissed. Apollo's eyes remained in motion, considering closets, stairs, doors, pathways. The basement and his room were obvious hideouts. But were they too obvious? Was he being watched? Was he being robbed?

Focus. If they took the back door, they risked being seen scaling the backyard fence, which was visible from the kitchen window. If they took the front door, they might run into a parent at the mailbox. If they hid in the house, they might be trapped. Was that worse or better? Girls discovered in the basement sounded morbid; girls discovered in his bedroom sounded sordid. Would he even have a bedroom after that kitchen door opened?

"Apollo, I thought your parents worked until six," Sol said, breaking Apollo's trance.

"They do, normally," he said, rising from the table. He wasn't even sure if it was his mother or his father.

"Well, today isn't looking too normal," Sol sneered. "I hope you don't expect us to run out the back door like a pack of hoodrats."

"Hoodrats don't move in packs," Kai said, grabbing Zed and Sol's arms. "The scientific name for a pack of hoodrats is a step team."

Unsure whether to laugh or commit ritual suicide, Apollo stayed seated. It was easier to think while sitting down.

The kitchen door swung open as Apollo's father entered with shopping bags.

"Ohhh, playa playa," his father said with a wide grin, his voice booming over the air conditioning, the closing garage door, and his own thunderous footsteps. A shoulder nudge swung the kitchen door shut, and within seconds, he had decamped to the master bedroom, not even stopping to greet their guests. His presence hung in the air, though, his cologne thick and musky, his silence filling the vacuum. Apollo felt dazed.

Sol spoke. "Bruh, your dad is African as fuck," she said.

"What do you know about Africans?" asked Zed.

"Enough to get a good tip," Sol said with a snicker.

The snicker snowballed into a deep, fulfilling laugh that rumbled through the room, dropping shoulders, slackening jaws, loosening backs. Apollo felt pure joy tickle its way up his stomach and into his throat, escaping into the air only to respawn in his stomach moments later. Zed pounded the table, Kai cupped her mouth, Sol rolled on the floor.

Apollo recovered first, glancing at the clock. 2:16. Why couldn't an entire day feel like the past four minutes?

"So, to answer Zed's question," he said, "there is no way anyone will get hurt. The satellites will burn as soon as they drop out of orbit. That's how they make satellites these days, to reduce pollution and prevent espionage. And none of these satellites serve any purpose other than surveillance. I triple-checked."

Sol rose from the floor. "Okay, you've answered all our questions about the details of the plan, but what's the purpose? Theo wanted to shit on his old job. I get that. I want to shit on my current job. But what's this about? What does this do for us? We're already legends."

"We're not legends," Zed said. "No one really knows why we did what we did back in June. The hashtag was a joke, and beyond a few activists, it's been forgotten. I followed it on social all summer. If we do this, they still won't know why, but they'll at least know we made our mark."

Apollo nodded. Zed was starting to understand the vision. He doubted she believed, though. She was so hung up on collateral damage and accidents, as if accidents were even possible with his level of organization. He'd encrypted their phones, anonymized their devices, scrambled IP logs, created scores of fake profiles for every single time he'd had to hit the forums for know-how. He had a VPN inside of his VPN, paid for with a cryptocurrency that didn't even have a name. And they still hadn't been caught after the tag on Stone Mountain. If that wasn't legend status, what was?

"You sound like Theo," Sol said, twirling a lock in her finger. "We desecrated a Confederate monument. *The* Confederate monument. Desecration is my shit, you know this. But you have to admit that this is extra."

"It's not extra, Sol," Zed said. "It's the real moment. We can't go around tagging our whole lives. That's extra."

A spiteful click skeeted from Sol's teeth. "Bitch, we're graffing, like, two weeks from now. Extra is your life." She laughed.

Apollo watched Zed closely. When she felt embarrassed or defeated, she produced the tiniest sigh, a whiffed huff that pressed the air like a kiss. He hadn't heard it yet, but she looked flustered. Maybe she really did believe. Maybe he should speak.

"Bitch, I hate you," Zed finally snorted.

Apollo's face collapsed into his palm.

Kai sighed and rose from the table. "Zed," she said, "You still trying to play today? I finally got a new racket, and I'm not trying to hear y'all argue like we're not already all in this shit. I've gone a month without group chat and dick. Real, extra, legendary, *I don't give a fuck.* This is the last summer before we're boring. The purpose is to make it count." She turned to Sol. "Bitch, you happy now?"

Apollo sniggered as Sol nodded begrudgingly. Kai went to retrieve her shoes from the foyer.

"Yeah, I'm out," Zed answered, following Kai. "You need a ride, Sol? I know you hate Kenwood, but I can drop you off first."

"Nah, I'm going to chill with this goober for a bit," Sol said. "Not much going on at home right now. I cleaned it up a few weeks ago. The less time I spend there, the cleaner it stays. Plus, my bike isn't fitting in your car."

"Suit yourself," Zed said, flashing Apollo a raised eyebrow. The front door opened and closed in a blink.

Apollo watched Sol twirl her hair, her fingers aimlessly coiling her wavy strands. She watched him back. He brandished his phone and scrolled mindlessly, the silence thickening between them. An Ars Technica article on the "internet of things" drew his attention. The article's provocations made him scan the room, avoiding Sol. His parents relied on him to set up all the devices they were constantly ordering, just as he depended on them to innovate ways to move between systems. Between the living room, dining room, and kitchen, they had a smart TV, a smart blender, a smart clock, and a smart vacuum; he'd hacked them all. Had he missed anything?

He glanced in Sol's direction, avoiding her glare. She was still watching him. Why was she here? Why was his dad here? He again found his face ensconced in his palm.

"You never answered my question," she finally said. "I know my friends. Zed loves a challenge, Kai loves Theo, Theo loves to do the right thing. But you, no one knows what you think, what you want. Zed thinks she knows, Kai doesn't care, and you won't tell Theo, but unlike them, I know what I don't know."

The invisible hand of circulating air suddenly caressed Apollo's skin, producing a slight shiver. Or was that Sol giving him chills? Why hadn't she asked him what he loved? Did she think so lowly of him that she couldn't even imagine him feeling love?

"You really need to learn how to respond to direct questions," Sol said. "Especially if we get locked up for this shit."

"I was thinking," Apollo said.

"Learn how to think and talk. I'm not here for my health."

"Why are you here then?"

"Why is your dad home this early?"

"What does that have to do with anything?"

"Nothing. I'm just letting you know how obvious it is when you avoid a question."

Apollo sighed. It annoyed him how right she could be, how purposeless their antagonism was, but how real it felt. The circulating air suddenly felt hot, his forehead throbbing.

"We're doing this because there's nothing else to do," he replied.

"What do you mean?"

"Think about our futures, all of us. We'll go to school, graduate, get jobs, buy cars to drive to the jobs, keep the jobs to pay for the cars, buy houses, get married, have kids, and then die. Because America. But like, what is that?"

"That's one way to do it. I already have a house, though, so I guess I'm American as fuck."

"This is serious, Solara. Think about what we know. We'll never have time other than now to act on it, to do something that matters. We'll be too busy thinking about credit scores and commute times and vacation spots. You have a house now, but you don't really care. You're gonna just have one or two gap years and then fall in line like the rest of us. Believe me. My parents were raised by rebels in the Biafran War. Look at them now. All they do is work and buy bullshit."

Sol sucked her teeth and stood up. "I'm going home," she said. "You coming?"

"What for?"

"Because you still haven't answered my question."

Apollo laughed and grabbed his shoes.

o o o

"Where'd you get this one?" Apollo asked as he mounted Sol's bike pegs.

"The streets!" Sol shouted as she pushed off. Apollo was impressed by how easily she carried his weight.

"If I told you that you biked like a maniac, would you care?" Apollo asked as his feet transitioned from bike peg to asphalt.

"If I told you that I cared about your opinion, would you believe me?" Sol replied.

Apollo scowled and followed her inside her house, taking it in for the first time. The living room was strewn with tools, emptied paint cans, and rolling papers. Neat stacks of boxes hugged lavender walls, a paint-splattered tarp sprawled over the carpet, and a fan spun furiously from the ceiling, its dangling cords scatting arrhythmic jingles. Apollo sank into the couch and compared the IRL experience to what he had glimpsed on Snapchat. It was smaller than he expected, much hotter, too, but it felt pretty homey, all things considered. But homes were still a distraction, property an illusion.

"Geez, I know it's messy, but tell me how you really feel," Sol said, entering with glasses and a jug.

Apollo slackened his scowl; it had apparently deepened. "Oh god, is this your infamous tea?" he asked.

"Infamous and ice-cold. You can take it or leave it."

Apollo took it and nursed down a gulp. It was good. He tilted his glass upward.

"You're welcome," Sol said, filling her own glass then plopping onto the couch. The jug dropped to the carpeted floor, producing a weak, sploshy thud.

Apollo eyed the sweat of the jug, aware of Sol's proximity to him. The couch was ample, as was the space between them, but he felt the heat from her legs, smelled the brine of her sweat. What was in this tea? He found himself scrutinizing his glass. The tea was the same color as Sol's skin. Was it just as sweet?

A blanket landed on his lap. "You wouldn't last in jail, man," Sol said. "You're too secretive about what you want. I don't know what it's like for guys, obviously, but when I would feel the urge, I just had to do it." Sol's socked foot began to hover over the blanket. He felt his pulse in his eyes as he watched her mimic stroking herself, legs splayed. "If you didn't own that shit, they owned you." Apollo watched her other foot dangle over the opposite arm rest. Her legs were quite long, he observed. "They already own your time; you can't give them your fucking desire, too." Apollo nodded, his pulse suddenly perceptible from beneath the blanket, his lap a morass of heat and sweat and pressure.

In one motion, Sol's legs snapped forward, sending her springing from the couch. She looked down at Apollo, a bemused look on her face. "You still haven't answered my question," she said.

Apollo stood up too. "Which one?" he stammered, the blanket dropping to the floor.

"Why are you so sure this is what we should do? I haven't even been to jail. I was just in juvie. And it was the worst year of my life. Trust." They stood face to face.

"I'm sorry," Apollo said, matching her gaze. Her skin was still hot; he could sense it.

"Yeah, me, too. I should have just tagged that bitch's car. But I had to get extra with it."

"Extra is life, though, right?"

Sol laughed, but her eyes remained still. "Extra is Zed's life."

"What's your life?" Apollo asked. "This house? I know you loved your grandma, but I don't get it. We're supposed to get houses, go to school, have kids, repeat. We're not supposed to be the siege engine that destroys the means of control. I thought stepping out of bounds was what the Celestials were all about?"

Sol scoffed and sat back on the couch. "Siege engine? Nigga, what? I'm gonna ignore that and start by saying you know I'm all in, but there's no way you really think what we're about to do changes things for real for real. For Kai, this is just the final summer excursion. Zed, too. They're thinking about college. You're all going to college!" She reached down for her glass and the tea jug.

Apollo watched the liquid stretch from the jug to the glass. "I might go, I might not, but it's not our job to think about this," Sol said. "That's my point. We're supposed to be fucking and eating fast food. That's actually what we would all do after a tag. Tag, hit the Wendy's, hit the 'Gram, hit the sheets."

"Were Jerry and Zed a thing?" Apollo asked.

Sol guffawed. "I knew you were a petty nigga," she said, offering a dap.

Apollo pushed her hand away. "Well, were they?"

"Maybe. Not my place to say. And we didn't hit the sheets that much, honestly. Mostly hit the jays."

Apollo lowered himself to the floor and sat cross-legged, leaning back onto his hands. "Fuck," he huffed. The fan cords jingled above him, snaking into clangs. Sol passed him the jug.

"Being small is hard, man. But you make it work. I know that owning a house doesn't guarantee shit. I work at a fucking Waffle House, and I make just enough to cover bills and blunts. If the roof falls or I get robbed, my only hope is that Old National gets gentrified. You guys will be in school, and my family is waiting right outside for me to fuck up, so all I can count on are luck and the impossible."

"I'm sorry," Apollo said.

"I'm good. Uncertainty doesn't scare me."

"It scares me."

"You seemed fine when your dad got home early."

"Yeah, but I won't let that happen again."

Sol shook her head and stretched across the couch. "That was one thousand percent not the right answer."

CHAPTER 14
AUGUST 9
9:52 P.M.
88°F

Wet grass splattered onto Theo's exposed legs as he shook his soiled sneakers. The slimy texture disgusted him, but his legs were cooled by the grass's moist touch. He leaned onto the handles of his lawn mower and surveyed the yard. It looked good, he thought, the trimmed rows almost perfectly aligned, just like his dad had taught him. He was only halfway finished, but he already felt the pride of a job well done.

A crack of thunder interrupted his moment of glory, reminding him that he was being rained on. Theo revved up the mower and started a new row, pleased that he had attached the receptacle bag at the last minute. "Pros always prepare for the worst," his dad said. Theo agreed. Raking and bagging wet grass was certainly the worst.

He marched across the yard, pushing the mower and watching for rocks and turtles. He couldn't see his forearms in the faint light provided by the Browns' porch lamp, but he knew they'd gotten bigger, stronger. When he'd first started cutting grass full-time, he couldn't grip the shaky mower without his forearms shaking as well. Now, enlarged and more defined, they remained steady, immune to the machine's constant shakes.

The rain was cool, but the humidity was suffocating. Theo looked forward to reaching the edge of the Browns' expansive yard and collecting his pay. *Maybe the thirty-five-dollar flat fee should be renegotiated*, he thought. Some of the yards on his route took ninety minutes to cut. He wouldn't get his car fixed before school if he kept losing so much time.

"Hurry the fuck up!" Mr. Brown shouted from the porch. Theo nodded and continued mowing, anxious to get home. Pushing the mower away from the porch, he continued toward the edge of the yard to finish the row. When he turned around to begin the next row, Mr. Brown was on the lawn, five yards away, barefoot and draped in a pristine white bathrobe. Theo silenced the mower, hoping Mr. Brown wasn't about to ask him to trim the edges. He'd left the edger at home.

Mr. Brown was close enough to speak at a normal volume, but he shouted as if he were still on the porch. "Theo, you're fired! This night-shift lawn mowing is fucking ridiculous! I'm trying to sleep." Theo groaned. He could feel the sass slithering down his tongue, but he was too tired to commit.

"Okay, Mr. Brown. Should I at least finish up? I only have a few rows left, and I'm collecting the full fee whether I finish or not." Theo smiled, pleased with his tiny act of resistance.

Mr. Brown crossed his arms, shifting his weight onto his left foot. Though his hands were stowed under his armpits, Theo could clearly see that his fists were tightly clenched. Theo's smile dissipated at the thought of having to fight a grown man. The small amount of muscle that he had built through tennis was concentrated in his shoulders and calves. There wasn't even a *One Piece* character with a fighting style suited for such an odd physique. Theo gripped the mower handles, comforted by the strength of his forearms.

Mr. Brown stared back at him. "Nigga, I have to work tomorrow. Here's fifty," he said, tossing a clump of cash onto the ground. "Come back when your business hours are convenient for the fucking customer," he muttered, turning away and heading toward his house.

Theo's grip slackened. This was triumph. Sort of. It wasn't really clear whether or not he was supposed to finish the yard. Theo decided to just take the money and leave. The rain stopped.

Maybe this is a sign, Theo thought as he walked home, pushing the lawn mower past houses with odd brick facades. Operation Dead Presidents hadn't been going as he planned anyway. He needed two thousand dollars to get the Civic repaired and repainted. He'd initially thought the plan was flawless. His dad would put up seven hundred, and Theo would bank the remaining thirteen hundred. But after a month, he'd only raised five hundred bucks. He had five weeks left before school started. At this rate, by that time, he'd have a little over one thousand dollars. He would definitely have to raise his base rate. He could tell everyone it was because of gas. Gas prices and taxes seemed to touch a special nerve with adults.

Theo entered the house through the garage door, kicking off his soiled shoes before entering the kitchen. A stack of mail awaited him on the counter: the most recent *Fader* magazine, his AP exam scores, a financial aid letter from Clemson. The envelope for the financial aid letter had been opened.

Theo removed the letter and scanned it. One of his scholarships had been canceled due to criminal charges being brought against a major donor, so sixteen thousand dollars would have to come out of pocket until the shortfall could be fixed. "Jesus," Theo said aloud. Disoriented, he grabbed the *Fader* and the AP exam scores and slinked up the stairs toward his bedroom.

Sixteen thousand. Six-ten thousands. One hundred sixty hundreds. Shadowing him as he dressed for bed, the sum bounced around Theo's mind, its very precision somehow making it harder to fathom. Theo turned on his bed lamp then flopped onto the bed, exhaustion coursing through his body. Despite his fatigue, lying in bed only made him feel more restless.

Theo grabbed the *Fader* from his nightstand. A portrait of some band he'd never heard of was plastered on the cover. The odd trio sullenly stared back at him. Theo closely examined the haircut of who he assumed to be the lead singer. She had a blond bob with shaved sides and streaks of cinnamon red. "I'm guessing either electropop or folk house," Theo joked aloud.

Theo dropped the magazine on the floor and grabbed his phone, opening his YouTube app and searching for the music of the mystery band. Theo laughed as soon as he heard the bubbly synths and cheery lyrics of the band's lead single, "Born to Dance."

"The bob don't lie," Theo said to himself, closing the app with a victorious smile. Instinctively, his fingers scrolled to his text messaging app. Kai had been silent for nearly a month. Theo knew what it meant, but he still found himself primed to talk to her as if it had only been hours since they'd last spoke. He stared at their message history, his thumb unmoving. The phone's LED display stared back then blinked off.

Theo dropped his phone to the floor and rolled over, turning off his lamp. He dreamed of numbers, disembodied numerals floating around him like the number of the day on *Sesame Street*. There was something intimidating about the numerals, so Theo ran from them. Relentlessly, they pursued him, drifting through walls and floors and glass and trees like apparitions. Cornered, Theo began to add the numbers, his hands flailing as he carried ones and twos and sixes and fours. As he added them, they decreased in number but increased in size. Eventually one remained, metastasized into some behemoth integer that enveloped Theo like a blob, suffocating him.

Theo awoke to two voicemails. One was from his father: "Hey son, I saw your letter from Clemson. State school looks pretty damn appealing right now, but I want you to get out of Georgia, see a little more of the world. I never told you this, but I set you up a college fund just in case something like this happened. It's yours, son. You earned it. See you at dinner."

Theo couldn't believe his dad was counting South Carolina as "the world." He couldn't even name a rapper from South Carolina. Still, a warm calmness settled over him, his body feeling limber. He played the second voicemail. It was from Mr. Brown: "I paid you in advance, so you better finish the job. I don't care about how fucking hot it is. If my grass isn't cut by the time I get home today, I'm going to knock that stupid smile right off of your high yella face. I know where you—"

Theo erased the voicemail, wondering whether Mr. Forrester would categorize Mr. Brown as shouting or yelling. Holding his phone above his head, he scrolled over to the weather app. The forecast was unbearable: no clouds, 100 percent humidity, 94ºF. "Feels like 105ºF," the app taunted. Theo sighed, leaning over the bed to fish Mr. Brown's payment from his rain-soaked shorts. A refund was the only option.

Suddenly, he resolved to get a job at the mall. He'd still cut grass, but if his dad was fronting all of his college fees, Theo wasn't going to take his seven hundred to get the car fixed, especially when he'd lied about how it got damaged in the first place. He'd raise it all himself. The plan was solid. Air-conditioned days, warm nights, a month of dignified, legit work. Theo could feel the guilt evaporating from his conscience. He'd make this right.

He showered quickly, the soap skating over his skin like water skis on packed snow. He was dressed as soon as he was dry. Stopping to make sure he looked presentable, he scanned himself in his bedroom mirror: khakis, black shirt, black dress shoes, black tie. "You clean up nicely," Kai would probably say, though neither of them ever could figure out what the hell that meant. Leaning in closer, he examined his face, running his hand over his cheeks and rejoicing in the faint layer of stubble that had started to emerge a few days earlier. He couldn't wait for it to grow thicker so he could shave it off and finally wear some of the aftershave his uncles always gave him for Christmas. He'd picked the bottles up so many times that he knew their weights just as well as he knew their smells.

The garage was ablaze. As soon as Theo opened the door, the hot air crashed into his face; it felt like he was being slapped by someone with fresh pancakes for hands.

The Civic was even hotter, the stale, sizzling air liquefying the grease he'd smothered into his crescent waves. Theo groaned and grabbed a towel from the glove box, wiping away the oil. Always prepared for the worst. Casually, he started the car and pressed the garage door opener at the same time, exhilarated by the fact that for the first time in two weeks, he was driving somewhere that wasn't the gas station or Food Depot.

Theo sped toward Mr. Brown's mailbox, opening it and tossing in an envelope with cash and a messy apology note. He sped away just as quickly, swearing he'd seen the blinds move.

South Cobb Drive was as busy as he'd expected, cars swerving in and out of an unending patchwork of sprawling plazas, gas stations, fast-food joints, and crusty apartment complexes. Theo was relieved when Cumberland Parkway finally appeared; it wasn't much different, but at least its plazas had stores he liked.

Cumberland Mall appeared soon after. Theo parked near the food court, grabbed his resume, and hopped out. He headed toward the entrance. Entering the foyer, he shuddered as a blast of air conditioning enveloped his body. He could feel his summer being redeemed.

He walked the mall, considering his options. Food court? Too real. GameStop? Too loud. American Eagle? Too white. Aeropostale? Too black. Sears? Too old. Express? Too EDM. H&M? That could work.

He strolled inside, greeted by some Taylor Swift remix that he recognized but felt a desperate need to pretend he'd never heard. Herds of fifteen-year-old girls swarmed about, yanking clothes off the racks and shelves as their trailing mothers publicly frowned and privately shopped on the H&M website from their phones. "This is cute!" repeatedly erupted from unseen mouths, thickening the overly perfumed air.

Intimidated by the line at the cash register, Theo decided to flag down an employee. Strategically, he darted to the men's section, a lonely wall lining the back of the store. The men's merchandise was neatly organized, nearly untouched. A plump Latina with bunned hair asked if he needed help. "Yeah, I'm thinking about applying to work here. What are hours like?"

The woman peered back at him through purple contact lenses, studying him. "You're not one of those secret shopper auditors, right? You have to tell me if you are."

"I'm not an auditor, but I'm pretty sure I wouldn't have to tell you. That would defeat the purpose of conducting a secret audit. Should I speak with someone else?"

She turned her head, scanning for potential eavesdroppers. Theo studied her bun as her neck swiveled, wondering how it could remain so perfectly still, frozen in place like frosting on a birthday cake. "No, we're good," she finally answered, guiding him over to a rack of acid-green T-shirts and pretending to offer him fashion advice.

"So, here's the deal. We get mad hours, but the manager is, like, insane. Like, literally insane. Without sanity. She doesn't have it." Her outstretched arm was suddenly frozen, pointing toward the hideous green shirts as if she'd found the perfect visual representation of the manager's mental health. Theo raised his eyebrows, encouraging her to continue.

Her arm regained consciousness, limply dropping to her side. "She only hires people who either look Puerto Rican, run really fast and can prove it, or who, like, went or are going to business school. And if you betray her, she will literally ruin your life. I knew this one girl—"

"Where is she?" Theo interrupted. The woman gasped, grabbing Theo's shoulder and squeezing tightly. Theo stared back at her blankly.

"Sorry," she said, her stubby hand still on his shoulder. His dick fluttered in his pants, unsure whether he was excited or afraid. "I thought I heard her footsteps. I feel like she's everywhere sometimes," the woman whispered, scanning the store again and pointing toward a short, dark-skinned woman standing near the store entrance. Theo had missed her on the way in.

He walked toward the manager, the woman's hand sliding down his back like an iron on cloth. "You've got nice shoulders," she said as he walked away.

Her paranoia clung to him as he approached the manager, summoning memories of his impromptu meetings with the Loss Prevention department at Six Flags. They'd only approach him when he was in a group, singling him out, marking him. The conversations never varied. "Anything you want to tell me?" one of them would inquire as if Theo were a regular informant. There were always two of them: one asking questions, one just there.

"No," he'd answer.

"You sure? We've got cameras, but you're our eyes and ears," they'd say, pointing skyward, their outstretched arms revealing vermillion armpit stains.

"Yeah," Theo would say, walking away alone, his coworkers gone.

The only conversation that hadn't followed that script was the one informing him he was being fired.

"Theo Santos?" an Asian man in shades had asked, stopping Theo in the middle of a trip to the restroom. Theo knew the guy was affiliated with Loss Prevention; his voice was so polite that it was accusatory. All of his questions were propositions.

"Yeah?" Theo had replied.

"What would you say if I told you I've got footage of you seeing but not reporting internal theft? You do know that internal theft is our largest source of loss, right? You do know that if you see something but you don't say something, you're enabling loss, right?" Theo stared at the man, unsure of what he was getting at. The man had stared back at him, calm. "This is your last chance," he had told Theo.

"For what?" Theo asked.

"To be responsible." Theo laughed. He'd been to work on time every day, humoring customers, never taking long breaks, standing in that hot-ass sun.

"Okay," Theo said, walking away. Five steps later, he was surrounded by a gaggle of Loss Prevention goons who quickly escorted him to his locker on the outskirts of the park. They didn't even let him piss before he was walked to his car.

The manager was obviously from New York City, her tone nasal and fierce, words flowing out of her like water from a faucet. Theo could easily imagine her leaving a voicemail on a Dipset mixtape or speaking trilled Spanish on some Vince Staples song. He introduced himself and handed her his resume. She shook his hand firmly, her eyes flitting between his resume and his torso like she was comparing a high-resolution photograph to its thumbnail.

"No retail experience," she said with finality, as if they had been debating. "Why should I hire you to be the steward of my customers' experiences?"

Theo mulled over her words. *Steward of customers' experiences.* What the fuck did that mean? Remembering the employee's tips, he improvised an answer. "I would be a great steward of customer experience because I am light on my feet, as evidenced by my tenure at Six Flags, and I am a business major, so I am very interested in business holistically, not just the management stage," he stammered, proud of himself for using words like "tenure" and "holistically" outside of the terrible, weed-fueled poetry he wrote when he was bored.

"Hmm," the manager said, staring toward the store entrance and greeting an incoming stream of moms and tweens. "You're hired," she declared. "Report in on Monday at 8 a.m. with your birth certificate, ID, Social Security card, and a full H&M outfit. Including socks," she said robotically. "I will check your socks," she assured him. "Be on time or be jobless," she added, stepping away to help a mob of white girls who were overflowing with shopping bags, the weight of their purchases making their taut, tanned skin visibly sag.

Theo pulsed with satisfaction. His dad would be proud. Now all he had to do was find some work clothes. The manager approached him as he browsed the solitary wall of men's clothes. "I forgot to ask about your availability," she said, swaying toward him like a leopard stalking a hare. "I only hire people who can commit at least six months. Part-time work results in part-time customer experiences," she hissed. Theo could see the crazy, but he told himself it was just eccentricity.

"Yeah, I'm taking classes at, um, Oglethorpe, so I'll be around."

She exhaled loudly. "Thank you, Theo," she said, walking away. Theo smiled. This job would be fun.

Gliding through the mall, beaming confident smiles at girls he hoped were old enough, he found himself in an electronic goods store, browsing. A lifeless employee followed him out of duty more than suspicion, his eyes pendulating like some robotic Cheshire cat.

Theo eventually stopped browsing to fiddle with the knobs on a sleek radio that looked like it should have been a projector or an atomic clock or a router— maybe even all three at once—but was nonetheless just a radio. He had little knowledge of Atlanta's radio stations. He exclusively played music from his iPhone, his dad exclusively listened to wholesome jazz CDs, Apollo exclusively listened to news podcasts, Kai exclusively listened to awful Spotify playlists, and Sol exclusively never drove. Except for that one time she'd crashed his car into the gate of a former military base. Yeah, that wouldn't be happening again.

Theo settled on 90.1, the only radio station he knew, courtesy of Zed. It was the afternoon, so the NPR member station played its local content. A clear voice droned into his ears, bland yet mesmerizing. He could see why Zed was addicted. Noticing that the employee was still slavishly focused on him, almost against his will, Theo began pacing the radio aisle, helping the employee stir.

The member station reported on the aftermath of #FireandBrimstoneMountain, the lives affected by the fires from that night, the singed bird carcasses that littered people's yards. Theo felt slighted that they didn't say "*hashtag* Fire and BrimStone Mountain." *Radio's just too old-school to get that,* he assured himself. The soothing voice of the reporter eventually gave way to the sound of crackling fire, recorded from the night of the tag. Theo always referred to it as the tag, but he secretly felt it had been something more than another night of running through Cabbagetown or Piedmont Park or East Point. The sputtering roar of the flames penetrated his psyche, demanding that he call the tag something else, something more destructive, more sinister.

"Terrorism is unacceptable, and I pray the culprits behind this heinous act are brought to justice," a Stone Mountain homeowner, an elderly black man, barked with conviction, the flames still audible behind his voice. Theo thought of *Gone with the Wind*, recalling the scene where Sherman conquered Atlanta. A stark subtitle—"Sherman!"—flashed across the screen as flames enveloped the city. Apollo had always insisted that this was the only good scene in the movie; he even had a GIF of that scene that he sent to Theo every time the Falcons won, as if Atlanta could only be victorious when it burned. Theo was caffeinated with guilt, his heart hammering, his mind singularly focused on the tag. Jerry used to call tagging *bombing*, like an orthodox graffiti writer. Theo had always felt the term was a little over-the-top, but now it felt cuttingly precise.

He paced the aisle as the report continued, more homeowners describing scorched grass, felled trees. Their voices were indignant, pestered. Theo stood in place once the sound of the flames finally subsided, transitioning back to the hypnotic voice of the reporter. Theo exhaled, relieved as if he'd been huffing the smoke from the fires and was now breathing fresh air. The report concluded: "The FBI encourages all tips to go to senior agent Tilly Erickson. Please visit the WABE website for more details." Theo flicked off the radio, darting out of the store. He didn't even flinch as he exited the mall and plunged into the smoldering afternoon heat. The only heat he felt was from his phone, seething in his pocket, beckoning him to contact Tilly, to not taint this good day.

He had to come clean. They had fucked up. They had hurt people. Graffiti was inhuman, hurt inflicted on walls, shutters, doors, property, aesthetics. They had gone beyond graffiti.

But he couldn't snitch. There'd be no coming back from that kind of betrayal. Zed and Apollo might forgive him, visit him, but Kai would erase him, banish him with that unique Black Girl Magic, that ability to hate severely, completely, eternally, a product of generations of disloyalty. And Sol, she'd already taken the heat for him once, ramming her fists into their thieving private tennis instructor just because he'd asked her to. "I wish I could fight her," he'd told her, complaining about practices the instructor kept skipping, taking his dad's money. Sol had maintained that she was defending herself after the instructor had gotten upset during an intense one-on-one lesson, but Theo knew that she set up that Sunday afternoon session specifically to kick the instructor's fit black ass. Sol had lost her independence at Independence Park. *How ironic*, Theo always thought, unsure of whether it was irony or a coincidence. Sol had done that for him, out of pure friendship.

The interior of the Civic plunged him back into those crackling flames. He'd take the heat, all of it. He owed everyone for fucking up the night with his shitty planning, for not replanning once things started to—literally—go downhill, for not standing strong after they decided to go through with it, for not being honest with himself. He had started this, and he would finish it. Fuck Six Flags. Fuck H&M. Fuck Mr. Brown. He had real work to do.

He quickly found the contact number for Tilly Erickson and dialed it, sweat exploding out of his face. No one answered, but he left a long, detailed message, speaking slowly and clearly, energized by his newfound conviction. Finished, he cranked on the car, cracked the windows, and reversed out of the parking lot. Hot air swept his face as he blitzed through anxious Thursday traffic, but he didn't flinch. Apollo was right.

CHAPTER 15
AUGUST 10
8:16 P.M.
90°F

Zed loaded a box of paint cans into her car, wondering how the night would unfold. After closing the rear door, she turned around to catch the sunset, fuchsia streams lingering in the sky, resisting the inevitable darkness. Crows cawed in the distance, their primal screeches strangely calming. The garage door opened, but Zed didn't turn around. She knew it was her mom. When she approached people, her footsteps were always cautious, reluctant to interrupt, yet interrupting nonetheless.

"What are you doing tonight?" her mom asked, stepping into the driveway and peeking into the trunk of Zed's MINI. "Paintballing again?"

"No," Zed answered, turning away from the sunset to face her mother. "Tonight, I'm going on a street art tour."

"In Atlanta? That explains the sketchbook in the back."

"Yeah."

"Take some nice pictures! I hear that BeltLine is really beautiful, much prettier than the rest of the city."

Zed smiled, reaching to squeeze her mom's tan shoulder, which was exposed under a loose tank top. Her skin was smooth, recently lotioned. "Cities aren't supposed to be pretty, mom. They're just supposed to be livable." Zed's other hand snaked into her pocket, grasping the list of Safe Zone murals that she'd be visiting that night. The Graffiti Task Force would be busy tomorrow.

"Well, I'm out, Mom. Catch you later," Zed said, stepping in and out of an obligatory hug like a mannequin that swiveled on a single axis. Her mother kissed her forehead and returned to the garage, her slippered feet dragging across the garage floor, the true volume of her footsteps.

Zed texted Apollo when she reached his house, hoping his parents didn't come outside. She watched as lights flickered on and off throughout the house like it was some sort of oversized pinball machine. Apollo was looking for something. Zed tried to visualize him moving from room to room, but her memory of the house was too vague. She didn't mind if it stayed that way.

Eventually, the light for the foyer came on, followed by the porch light, and then Apollo, who dashed to the car, his backpack in tow.

"Hey," he said, swooping down to fit into the low car. "Sorry about that, lost my gloves." Zed nodded, pecking his cheek then pressing the gas.

Kai and Sol were ready outside of Kai's house, their exposed legs and arms shiny from obviously recent applications of Vaseline. Zed looked down at her paint-splattered skinny jeans and ratty black T-shirt and sighed internally. She was the only one who ever seemed to remember that they could get arrested for this. Maybe she shouldn't have always insisted that the Graffiti Task Force was a joke. It was, but their power was real.

"Don't worry, bitch. We've got real clothes," Sol said, climbing in through the passenger's seat and grinning widely. "We'd look pretty sus cruising around in sleeves and all black in mid-August, no offense." Zed smiled back through the rearview mirror. Kai climbed in behind her, visibly excited. After Apollo let the seat back and plopped back in, his head grazing the roof of the car as always, she drove off and exited the neighborhood.

Kai blurted her obvious secret before they'd even hit Highway 85. "Theo's coming!" she announced. Everyone shifted in their seats, eyes glued to the windows, suddenly interested in the town they constantly tried to escape. Kai continued, "He texted me today, apologizing for being all guilt-trippy and sappy, so I invited him along. He's going to meet us on Ponce."

"Cool beans," Sol muttered sardonically. Apollo was face-deep in his phone, so Zed focused on the road.

Kai had been the only person who was no longer cool with Theo. Their breakup—or whatever it was—had been understandable from both ends, but it was Kai who'd thought they'd *all* left him behind, as if their collective friendships had hinged upon a single relationship that they'd all always discouraged, including Kai herself. She used to openly mock Theo for blushing whenever she was around. "Do you have something you'd like to say to me?" she'd taunt, slapping his thigh, her hand puckishly close to his crotch.

But maybe it was everyone's fault. When they began planning their second bombing—Zed had decided they should start calling it "bombing" again, like Jerry always had—they didn't invite Theo along. He just seemed so devastated after the first time, it would be abusive to bring him along again, especially since they were scaling up. He wasn't about that life.

Kai had trashed Theo throughout July, especially as they planned for the second bombing, and no one had stopped her. She seemed to need it, it fueled her, but they all could have at least responded with something other than silence. Even with their reconciliation, which everybody saw coming, silence seemed to be their only answer. Sure, Sol's sarcasm was kind of a response, but even that was a form of silence— vocalized inaction, but inaction nonetheless.

The downtown skyline erupted into view from I-75/85 South. It wasn't impressive. It had always annoyed Zed that you could only see it best from the highway, as if the city planners knew it would lose its power if you saw it while standing still—which it did, whenever Zed found herself on a rooftop. But Zed still felt a sense of pride well up within her. This was her city. Even as a kid from the burbs, she felt an umbilical link to it, nourished by its heat, its energy, its music, its traffic.

"You should get over," Kai suggested, her head jutting between the headrests. Zed knew how to get there, but Kai loved navigating. Zed acknowledged her with a nod and merged right, needling through the traffic streaming in from I-20. Moments later, she was on Freedom Parkway, crossing over Boulevard.

"Who's going to say it?" Apollo queried, turning to peer into the back seat. Kai and Sol shrugged, so Zed spoke up.

"Boulevard," she said, mimicking Theo's nasally California properness, "What kind of street name is that? That's like naming a street, 'street'!" The car shook with laughter, the impression, as always, funnier than the joke. Zed hoped that Kai knew they were laughing with Theo, not at him.

Moments after turning onto Ponce De Leon, they pulled into a giant parking lot. They were early, so they sat in the car, watching people stream in and out of cars, gilded in sweat. The car was growing hot, but nobody seemed eager to jump out. This was Ponce, after all. Not really their scene. Or their tax bracket.

Theo pulled up grinning, windows nowhere in sight. Zed could feel everyone shudder when he rolled them up.

Zed found herself hugging Theo and everyone else as they stood in the parking lot, hot, static air crinkling between them. It felt good to be reunited. Zed and Sol had changed clothes during the ride into the city, their skin now covered by tight-fitting Under Armour shirts and dark tights, but they were still glowing.

Zed opened her trunk, removing the tattered blanket covering the box of paint cans. Everybody lined up, backpacks agape like catfish mouths, Zed unloading spray paint canisters and surgical masks. Apollo declined, his backpack zipped shut. Zed waved him away then stuffed some extra cans into her bag. He wasn't getting out of it tonight, especially since he'd brought gloves.

"So, where are we headed?" Theo asked Zed as they walked west on Ponce, collapsing into single file as they brushed shoulders with a homogenous mob of thirty-year-old white dudes who were desperately fighting to return to their twenties. They were all either bearded and bald or ponytailed and clean-shaven, sentient border disputes, Civil War reenactors forever loyal to the Confederacy of youth. Zed smiled as she heard the familiar yelp of a guy who'd rammed shoulders with Sol, expecting her to yield, because why shouldn't she? She was walking where he planned on walking. Sol never yielded.

"We're headed to Edgewood," Zed responded as the sidewalk cleared and Theo reappeared at her side. He nodded then fell back, leaving Zed alone to lead.

"What is all this shit?" Sol bellowed from a few feet away, rattling a young black woman who was jogging toward them with her dog, the fattest Doberman Zed had ever seen. Its ears were so plump that they drooped down, too heavy to stay in place.

"Ponce City Market," Apollo answered, his voice directed behind him. Zed stopped, turning around to find Sol planted in front of a towering brick building, the crew surrounding her, staring upward. The building was old, but it had a tacky sheen of recent interest, like an old vinyl record that had been dusted off and labeled "old," its age confirming its cool.

Apollo continued. "It's a redevelopment thing. Used to be a government building and was a warehouse before that. Now it's all yuppified and shit," he said coolly.

"Why do you know this?" Theo asked.

"I was looking at off-campus options for housing for junior year, and this was listed. Not my style or my budget, but apparently, it's a big deal. Supposed to provide residents with everything they need. Clothing stores, farmers market, bars, restaurants, art. You could probably live there and never have to come out."

"That sounds great to me," Theo said cheerfully.

"Sounds like jail to me," Sol said. Zed couldn't tell if she was joking or not.

"This is a haven. No one builds their own jail," Kai said, shooting Sol a smile.

"Pablo Escobar did," Apollo said, dryly. Zed rolled her eyes. Since the first bombing, Apollo had been oddly militant, delving headfirst into the biographies of lionized dissidents: Malcolm X, Pablo Escobar, Vladimir Lenin, Huey Newton, Assata Shakur. He was now overflowing with *facts*, mundane information that was uttered with bizarre reverence. It *mattered*, Apollo insisted.

"It was still a fucking jail," Sol retorted, walking away. Everyone laughed, even Apollo. They continued down Ponce, hitting a left on Glen Iris and heading south. Small talk came and went as the city bustled around them, cars screeching-stopping-going, people running, walking, biking. The heat was amplified by their harried pace. Rolling hills greeted them as they trekked past modest houses on the right and gleaming high-rises on the left. Zed resented the faux-rebellious wheatpastes featured on some of the houses, images of shadowy faces captioned with bland slogans: fight the power, green power, power to the people. If there was any paint remaining at the end of the night, she would be doing some throw-ups.

"Why didn't we park closer?" Kai asked, shimmying to the front of their procession where Zed was still leading.

"I didn't want our night to be too functional. We can be commuters when we're thirty," Zed said. Kai beamed, skipping a few steps ahead. Kai loved it when she was sassy. Zed liked it too, sometimes.

Theo joined her, leaving Zed alone, flanked by Apollo and Sol, who were uncannily chatty. Zed continued along by herself, watching Kai and Theo interact. They looked peaceful, but something was off. Theo hadn't complained about the heat a single time, and he'd been smiling since he stepped out of the car. Zed slowed her pace to allow Sol and Apollo to catch up.

"What's up with Theo?" she asked them, surprised to see that they were visibly annoyed by her interruption.

"I think he's happy to see us," Apollo offered, shrugging.

"I think he realized that pussies don't get pussy," Sol corrected him, also shrugging. A laugh rollicked Zed, catching her midstride, her legs nearly noodling beneath her.

"If you really believe that," Apollo said, unaffected by Sol's joke, "Let's invite him out tomorrow. At least this time around, he'll know what we're getting into."

"And he'll know he isn't in charge," Sol added. Zed remained silent, unconvinced that Theo's participation was even up for discussion. She trusted Theo, but Kai had shown her the text messages that had led to their breakup. For a month, he'd transformed all of their correspondence into a repository for his guilt. Their standard "good morning" text became a nightmare exchange, with Theo detailing his latest fiendish dream—often some bizarre mélange of Six Flags, cars, and columns of fire: a giant bonfire in the Six Flags parking lot, The Georgia Scorcher, a roller coaster, becoming a Transformer wreaking havoc in the city.

Other times, Kai would text him, "What u doing?" and he'd say, "researching," then send reams of links about the bombing, sometimes the same link over and over. The worst was when Kai would ask him to hang out. He'd insist that she drive, knowing she'd have to borrow her parents' car, claiming that he couldn't risk being caught in his car. The dude was shook.

Glen Iris morphed into Randolph Street as they crossed over Freedom Parkway. Ten minutes later, Randolph terminated at Edgewood, their destination. Theo and Kai crossed the street, nearly disintegrating as a herd of bikers dispersed and reformed to get around them, one biker shouting about the *obviousness* of the newly painted bike lanes. *They did have quite a gleam,* Zed thought, wondering if there was a brand of spray paint that could reproduce that civic glow.

After looking both ways, Zed, Apollo, and Sol joined Kai and Theo across the street, Zed reclaiming her position at the front of the pack as they headed west. Zed was glad to see that traffic was light. After a few blocks, they slinked into a gravel-strewn parking lot, the home of a mural of a giant smiling owl, beaming from the bricks of a peppy new building, an art gallery. Brown and yellow feathers adorned its meticulously drawn body, a concert of shadows, colors, curves, and edges. A lone streetlight illuminated the lot, which smelled of cheap beer and leaked coolant. Zed smiled back at the owl, arming herself with a rock, tossing it and shattering the light.

She dropped her bag and removed her sketchbook and her copy of the city's list of approved murals, verifying she was in the right place. This was the spot.

"So, this is it," Theo declared, a statement more than a question.

"This is grade-A street art," Sol said, sneering up at the giant owl. "The pride and joy of the great city of Atlanta, home of the street art revolution," she continued.

Everyone laughed except Apollo, who quickly responded. "I think it actually looks pretty all right. Owls are symbolically wise. This owl smiles. He doesn't let knowledge bring him down," he said.

Zed wasn't surprised.

"Hmm," someone said, probably Kai, declining to take the bait.

"This is my outline," Zed announced, flipping open her sketchbook and shining her cell phone light onto a drawing of Lorde Zed, her tag. The letters were three-dimensional, interlaced like fresh noodles, the illest tag Zed had ever drawn. It wasn't quite wildstyle, but she was pleased. She'd redrawn it dozens of times, rubbing her thumb-sized eraser into a pathetic pink speck. This was the third time she'd be slashing another artist's work, and it was sure to be her best work yet. She wanted the original artist to see this and remember her name forever. She was going to Sherman this motherfucker.

"How in the shit are we going to tag a twenty-foot wall?" Apollo asked, glaring at Zed. His tone was pesky, but she was pleased that he'd said "we." He was learning.

"With this," Zed said, coolly retrieving a rusted ladder that was stashed next to an oddly pristine dumpster. She was relieved that it was still there. A YouTube video from January had shown the artist, a quiet, spectacled young white woman, leaving the ladder on-site after a montage of her touching up the mural. At the time, Zed had wondered if that was a mic drop or an offer of generosity. Now the artist's intentions were irrelevant. The ladder was an opportunity, her opportunity.

"I think that dumpster would work better," Sol suggested. "It's probably more stable."

"Yeah," Kai seconded. Zed nodded, returning the ladder to the side of the building. Apollo and Theo followed her, placing their shoulders onto the dumpster. Zed noticed that they left a space between them. It was probably for Sol, but she confidently filled the slot, jumping in. "On three," she announced. They heaved in unison, the dumpster easily submitting. While Theo goofily flexed his arms to a disinterested Sol and beaming Kai, Apollo and Zed peeked inside. It was empty, not even harboring a smell.

"Must be new," Apollo shrugged. Zed didn't have any other theories, but she was jealous. Even the trash cans were clean on this side of town. She wished she could say the same about the rat-harboring dumpster located behind her uncle's apartment in East Point. The rats were so cozy in that dumpster, they didn't even scatter when it opened. With their noses cocked upward and their beady eyes brimming with expectation, Zed always imagined them saying, "About damn time." Her uncle agreed. He'd started calling taking out the trash "making a delivery."

Zed fetched her gloves, masks, and two white canisters from her backpack, tossing them onto the dumpster and then hoisting herself up. She paused to take in the view. There wasn't much to see, but even when Zed was only slightly elevated, she felt a calming clarity, a sense of enhanced understanding that was only accessible from certain heights.

Following the plan, Apollo and Kai scattered across the lot to stand guard, Theo following behind them. They didn't exactly fit the profile of Edgewood street artists. Sol was the only who remained. She and Jerry had been the ones who'd introduced Zed to graffiti, so they always tended to oversee any complicated tags. Zed didn't mind. Sol always had good advice. Or hilarious commentary.

"I think you might need this," Sol said, placing Zed's sketchbook onto the dumpster. Zed smiled. Sol was never unreliable, in character or in deed.

Snapping on her gloves, Zed moved quickly, sketchbook in her right hand and a canister in her left. A familiar sweat began to form on her fingers as she pressed down on the tip of the canister, the heat of the night and the moment magnified by the gloves' tight fit. But Zed felt calm as the hiss of the canister and the shimmer of the paint gripped her, narrowing her focus. Slowly, the owl began to disintegrate before her eyes, feathers unraveling, its plumage dissolving in a spray of white mist. Zed's hand moved steadily, patiently, her eyes darting back and forth between her sketchbook and the wall.

The outline complete, she flipped up her surgical mask to catch her breath. The air was fuming, but she gulped it down, jumping off the dumpster.

Sol nodded, clearly impressed. Zed stood beside her, examining the outline from a distance. *This honestly could do without color*, she considered, quickly rejecting that same thought. She had to see it through as envisioned; each line and shade and hue had to materialize onto that wall exactly as planned.

"I've got a plan, Zed," Sol said, "I'm not going to do college or the military. I need stability right now. It helps me stay calm, you know? I'm gonna try to get a real estate license, fix up houses. Nothing major, but it's just for me, I think." Zed almost patted her on the back, but remembering her paint-covered hand, left it floating behind her. Sol eyed her quizzically, adding, "Stability also means staying single, sorry." They laughed. Zed was pleased to be her confidante. It was a first. She sensed something was being omitted, but declined to push it. Sol always pushed back.

"That's dope," Zed said.

"That's all you have to say? Just gave you my goals and you're looking at me like I'm a guidance counselor on a Friday afternoon."

Zed chuckled. "I just admire you. I'm about to go to college just because that's what I'm supposed to do, but you're actually thinking about all this shit."

"I've had plenty of time to think about things. And honestly, I didn't even used to think about the future. Well, I did, but I didn't think about it like I should have. I forgot how hard it is for people to change."

"What do you mean?"

"Now's not the time."

Apollo, Kai, and Theo began to return to the dumpster, but Zed waved them back to their perches. Such awful timing. Sol was finally opening up.

"You sure?" Zed asked.

"Yeah, finish this shit up. It's hot as hell out here."

Zed hopped back onto the dumpster, her backpack at her feet alongside the sketchbook. This time, a blueprint wasn't needed. Streams of blues and purples and yellows flared from her fingertips, coats upon coats of colors. She strafed across the dumpster, barraging the wall with paint. After forty minutes, her arms were slack, her shoulders searing with thorough fatigue.

Triumphant, Zed hopped off the dumpster a second time, summoning the last fragment of energy left in her body to push the dumpster back to its original position, alone. She joined Sol again, this time greeted by a wide belly slap. It stung, but it felt appropriate as Zed looked at the disfigured owl, its torso and lower face devoured by her tag, that beaming smile replaced with Lorde Zed, the stylized letters looking like demented braces. Apollo, Theo, and Kai returned again, bearing telling smiles. Zed's arms were too tired to throw into the air, but she flung them anyway, their limp fall even more effective than she'd hoped. No one said anything, even Theo. A month of detailed planning and research, and he was just getting invited along because Kai wanted him there, as if his absence in the past month had always solely been her decision and not a collective effort. "Sure," Zed said, responding as if Kai had been asking a question. She turned to Theo.

"This tag is amazing, Zed," he offered, his body language confident and eager. She knew Theo wouldn't let them down on purpose, but Zed could already feel the plan unwinding. She gripped the mural map in her pocket, withdrawing it and crinkling it in her fist. She walked to the dumpster and dropped it in, its pathetic plop drowned out by the screeching metal of the dumpster lid slamming shut.

"What was that?" Apollo asked.

"Nothing. Let's go home. I just saw some cops pass," Zed lied.

Despite her vexation, the journey back to their parked cars was fun. As they traversed Freedom Parkway, Theo decided to showcase his knowledge of his friends' favorite Atlanta songs. When he'd first arrived from California, he'd insisted on finding everyone's individual song. Everyone had a song, he'd sworn, leaving no one out, even Zed, who didn't even really listen to music. Queuing up a playlist on his phone, he streamed "Best Friend" for Sol, "Weeastpointin'" for Kai, "Bring Em Out" for Apollo, "Wrist" for himself, "Swing My Way" for Zed, and "Scotty" for Jerry. Everyone's song had been played in full by the time they reached the parking lot, but after they'd deposited their bags into Zed's trunks and hugged and dapped each other up, Theo lingered, looking at them expectantly.

"What?" Sol snapped.

Goofily, Theo pointed at the sky and started swaying. "Ki, ki, ki, ki," he chanted while launching into the dance, his strained voice echoing throughout the parking lot, scaring a shopper emerging from a yoga studio who dashed to his car. The rest of the crew immediately chimed in, Zed taking the backing vocals, Kai taking the ad-libs, and Apollo and Sol joining Theo for the verses. Minutes later, they were leaning on their vehicles, rollicked by continual bursts of spontaneous laughter. *Jerry would be proud,* Zed thought, another laugh seizing her, the promise of the night finally fulfilled.

CHAPTER 16
AUGUST 11
6:37 P.M.
94°F

THE WEATHER WAS FUSSY. IN A TWENTY-FIVE-minute span, Tilly had seen lightning bolts, sunlight, hail, and pure sky. It was annoying. More annoying than the ill-fitting Kevlar vest that loosely hung over her body. The custom-fitted vest had once been snug, but she'd lost too much weight, almost all of it from her breasts. Despite living in a city where even the deeply impoverished managed to avoid walking, Houndum demanded that all agents be intensely fit. She'd gone from running an eight-minute mile to a six-minute mile, her Coke-bottle physique melting into a tennis ball canister. She missed her bust, but it was nice to know that her body could still undergo change, could still morph.

Rick's enthusiasm was unchanged. He drove patiently, accommodating every driver who wanted to merge, pass, honk, or tailgate. The driver's seat was tilted at an absurd angle, the back of the seat almost touching the passenger seats behind it, but Rick sat arrow-straight, his spine a yardstick.

"How do you feel about Ciara?" Rick asked.

"No opinion," Tilly sighed. Rick was convinced that everyone cared about music as much as he did. He was wrong.

"But she's Ciara, child of Missy, mother of Future, *ex* of Future. She's like this generation's Erykah Badu," he pleaded.

Tilly remained silent.

"She's her own artist, of course, too," he added, extending his plea.

"Drive faster, Rick. I have shit to do."

"Sure thing, partner," he muttered, turning on his radio.

Tilly was surprised that he'd driven for this long with it off. *He must be really excited,* she realized. Her fingers grazed her vest. Bland trap music drifted from the speakers; the lead elements were unsubtle bass and a corny, ecstatic organ. The producer was probably from Gothenburg or Toronto, somewhere with health care. Tilly didn't recognize the rapper, undoubtedly some rando from some mixtape Rick would swear by this week and then condemn next week. She was annoyed that she knew it was trap music. But it was hard not to know when Rick was such a flowing faucet. He had a blog—he'd told her, multiple times, until she finally read it—but she'd only viewed it once, its thousands of posts too much to even consider parsing. There was something repugnant about being too immersed in the moment, too coated in the contemporary. There was also something fearless about drowning in the moment, something brave, but she had bills. Bravery was for college students and dogs.

Tilly's attention returned to the odd weather unfolding on South Cobb Drive. The sun was back, producing iridescent sparks that danced on the backs of the rain-splashed cars. Moments later, they pulled into a nondescript neighborhood filled with manicured lawns and expensive cars, mostly Escalades. She drove a Cadillac herself, but Escalades had always disgusted her. The name was too militant, upward mobility as siege.

Rick slowed his Lincoln Navigator to a crawl as they approached Theo Santos's address. The surveillance team had reported that Santos was the only one home, but Tilly didn't want any surprises. The music seemed to slow as well, but Tilly realized the song was actually just chopped and screwed, another genre she had learned about from Rick.

Rick parked the car in the driveway, and they stepped out slowly, their training and experience and fear muffling their footsteps, heightening their awareness. Tilly was sure that Santos wouldn't be a threat, but procedure didn't call for certainty. Since they had acquired the tag numbers for the Civic and the MINI Cooper from surveillance footage, they had been watching Santos and his friends for weeks while their arrest warrant was finalized. Other than their love for graffiti, they seemed normal, but that NSA agent had been right: normal teens didn't have encrypted emails and scrambled IP addresses. Something was up.

"I've always felt like no-knock warrants were made for people in apartment buildings. Everybody else has doorbells," Rick said as he mashed the doorbell.

"Rick, until about forty years ago, law enforcement never knocked on anything but skulls," Tilly sighed. "Especially for people of color," she added obligatorily, her hand on her holster.

The door swung open, Santos eyeing them. His clothing was oddly formal, Tilly noted. Dark slacks and a gray collared shirt clung to him like bedsheets. He looked like he was about to testify.

"Hi," Theo said politely, his voice cracking. "Are you the FBI?"

Rick laughed and stepped past him, entering a foyer with polished wooden floors. Tilly followed, her hand still resting on her holster. The house was cold.

"Yes, we are, kid. And I must say that's the friendliest greeting we've ever gotten," Rick answered as Theo closed the door, quietly leading them to the living room. Ornate cushioned chairs filled the room, their wooden backs curved like scorpion tails.

"Are you home alone?" Tilly asked.

"Yes, it's just me. My dad works late on Thursdays," Theo confirmed. "I didn't expect you to be black," he blurted.

"Now that's the regular greeting," Tilly teased.

"Is it really?" Theo asked.

"No, we don't normally greet people," Tilly said. "Sit down."

Theo sat, his hands in his lap, palms flat, supplicant. His compliance was annoying, Tilly decided. "Check his pockets," she commanded. Rick shuffled through them, extracting keys, a phone, and a portable fan. Theo smiled at her. Satisfied, Tilly cannily began to circle Theo's chair, Rick stepping in behind her.

Binary stars in orbit, they paced in cadence, steps synchronized. Rick spoke first.

"So, I'm pretty sure you know why we're here," he said.

"Yeah, I've got some information about the assault on Stone Mountain that happened earlier this summer."

"Why do you refer to it as an assault?" Rick asked, his pace slowing.

"Because it was done with the intention of hurting the city."

"Hurting the city," Tilly echoed, nudging Rick, who had stopped walking. "How do you know this?"

"Because I did it," Theo stammered.

"Why?" Tilly asked.

"Because I hate that mountain and what it represents."

"What does it represent?" Rick asked.

"Racism."

"Racism?" Tilly asked.

"Yeah, it has Confederate generals on it."

"It's also the home of a large black community, and the park is an employer of mostly black workers," Rick said.

"So was slavery," Theo retorted, his body loosening.

"You did this by yourself?" Tilly asked, ignoring his sarcasm.

"Absolutely."

"You, a seventeen-year-old tennis player and rap blogger from Anaheim, California, acquired the code-filled operations manual for a secret government satellite, entered a government facility, disabled the satellite's remote access panel, then entered an abandoned building in which only four people know the location for the server that connects to that satellite, bypassed that server's military-grade firewall, overrode the satellite's protocols, and utilized its onboard laser—also a secret—then escaped?" Rick now stood directly in front of Theo, leaning forward over him like a barber scrutinizing a hairline.

"Yes," Theo murmured.

"Okay," Rick said, the edges of his small mouth grasping for his ears. "We're going to have to take you in."

Theo outstretched his hands as Rick brandished a pair of handcuffs from his jeans. In one motion, Rick pulled Theo to a stand, clasped on the cuffs, a metallic wheeze gasping out as the restraints closed around Theo's wrists. Theo winced in response, his face collapsing into itself like an alarmed armadillo. Avoiding his pliant eyes, Tilly turned away, waving to Rick from over her shoulder and heading back outside. She paused as she opened the door to the SUV and watched Rick guide Theo in. She'd never arrested a teenager before.

After Rick closed the door, she tugged on his shirt and led him away from the vehicle. They stood on dry, brittle grass, its blades sharp, eager to prick. The sun was behind her, but Tilly still flicked down her shades before speaking to Rick.

"We both know he didn't do it alone," Tilly declared.

"Obviously."

"Then why are we taking him in?"

"Terrorism."

"Terrorism?"

"We solved it."

"We solved it?"

"Closed case."

"Closed case?"

"Are you just going to repeat everything I say?"

"Are you just going to act like this case isn't horseshit?"

"The case is solid. We tie him to Black Lives Matter, say he was radicalized online by WikiLeaks, say he's an identity extremist and that he loves Dead Prez, The Roots, Chief Keef, bang bang, done deal. Promotions, bigger offices, better cases. We bring this twerp in, and I guarantee we'll be collecting shitty Netflix documentary checks for life. Never bunt an underhand pitch, Tilly."

Tilly guffawed, stepping back to gulp down the hot air that was erupting from her throat. Rick was a careerist. Fucking Rick. Rick the Brick, immovable yet aerodynamic, chronic overworker, 93 percent closure rate no matter how minor or major the case, hoarder of vacation days, infrequent bather, online grocery shopper *because he didn't have time to shop in person.* Tilly shook her head hard in disbelief. Was this why he'd whiffed when Eric Sims had come by the office? *Or worse, had he arranged for Sims to come by the office?*

"Cutting corners isn't closing cases," she told him, her finger jabbing his shoulder.

"This case wasn't even meant to be closed. Houndum gave this to us on a broken wing and a whore's prayer."

"You're the whore, Rick, and you're not even a good one. You can't even recognize a good john. That kid is in over his head, and you're willing to exploit his fear because it *might* pay off. We both know it won't. A seventeen-year-old kid living in Marietta, Georgia, who graduated from Kennesaw Mountain High School, goes all the way to East Point, Georgia, thirty miles away, to destroy a racist monument thirty-five miles away when there's one fifteen minutes away? You know Kennesaw Mountain also has a Confederate memorial, right? And even beyond that, that same teenager individually has more coding knowledge than the two former hackers on his trail? Are you out of your fucking mind? That's the kind of fuckwit case that Dick Wolf wipes his ass with and then throws at the stupid intern who suggested it to him. Houndum sees a case like that, and we're back on the Eric Sims beat."

Rick glared at Tilly, a hot wind flicking at his loosened tie. She couldn't tell exactly what he was thinking. She felt bad. He'd been a model partner all this time, and his sole request for something selfish had been rejected. He was probably excited earlier because he'd had plans tonight. He'd finally figured it all out, put the puzzle pieces together all on his own, not in the way that they came out the box, but at least in a way that plausibly fit together. And she'd just trounced into the room and flipped the damn table.

Tilly was glad she'd brought her shades. She needed their steely cool, their unyielding opacity. He couldn't know she, too, was acting selfishly. She hated the idea of two black agents putting their names on a weak case.

"This is unnecessary, but okay, let's bring in the kid's friends, try to get them to confess, see what really happened, bring in a larger haul. But I reserve the right to change my mind, rein this all in. He lied to us, remember? Deal?" He extended his arm, his hand in a fist. Reaching out with her own fist, Tilly met it. Case closed.

"Did you guys just dap?" Theo asked as they climbed into the Navigator.

"You've got much bigger worries, kid. Sit back and shut the fuck up," Rick said, brandishing his gun for emphasis.

Alarmed, Tilly looked over at Rick. His gun already holstered, he was backing the car out of the driveway. She expected a smile of self-satisfaction, maybe even a grimace of irritation, but his face was emotionless.

Tilly's eyes settled on an air-conditioning vent as Theo's quiet neighborhood eased out of view. The road was too much to take in. She needed to keep things moving. The next move would be to call Natalie, the analyst she and Rick had assigned to watch Theo's friends. Natalie phoned her first, informing her that Theo's friends had gathered and were on the move, all of them wearing black. Exactly what Tilly didn't want to hear. Her hand was being forced.

"Rick, the other perps are on the move. We need to catch them while they're together. Natalie says they look like they're up to something. They're all wearing black."

"Other perps? I acted alone," Theo bleated from the back seat.

"Kid, cut the shit, we know your friends were at least your accomplices, maybe even the masterminds," Tilly told him, turning around to face him, raising her shades so Theo could see her irritation.

"My friends have nothing to do with this. They're probably wearing black because they're going to do some tags. They're artists. Artists wear black," he pleaded.

"Artists wear black. Kid, you are a fucking comedian. Too bad this isn't a stage. This is serious, okay? We know everything. We've been watching you for three weeks, you got that? Kaila, Zadie, Solara, Apollo, we know everything. Now either tell us what your friends are up to, or I will call in a fucking drone!" Tilly barked.

She looked over at Rick, hoping for at least the semblance of a smile. He always loved when they name-checked perps' friends and associates or threatened to call in a drone, almost always false threats, especially the drone.

Rick was unmoved, his eyes remaining on the road, his face blank. Tilly stared at Theo, eager to be relieved of this new role as an antagonist to teens and coworkers, a boss. There was something disturbing about how good it felt.

Theo mumbled an address, tears rinsing his bronze cheeks. "Thanks," Tilly said, turning around and entering the address into the Navigator's GPS, a touch screen installed directly into the console. *At least Rick buys himself nice things,* Tilly assured herself as the vehicle skated on I-285 South.

Natalie called again, asking for further instructions. "Maintain aerial support, Nat. And tell Houndum we're gathering up the remaining perps, and we'll be in later this evening. And be sure to tell him we're under budget." Tilly hung up, flinging her shades down over her face despite the fleet of clouds that was beginning to swallow the sun. Her mind was already considering decorations for her new office. Change was good.

CHAPTER 17
AUGUST 11
7:03 P.M.
94°F

THEO SAT QUIETLY AS HIS CAPTORS DROVE SOUTH down Highway 85. The handcuffs were wound tight, but at least they'd been nice enough to re-cuff him with his hands in front of him when they stopped for gas. Even the slightest movement of his wrists was excruciating. He'd never experienced such unceasing pain. But he'd rather feel that than the numbing panic that was slowly overtaking him as the car drove deeper into Clayton County, south of Atlanta. Pain was localized, but panic was all-encompassing, engulfing. Familiar parking lots and stores and restaurants were already transforming into places where he could concretely envision his death and nothing else, future crime scenes.

Theo only knew three addresses in Clayton County: Kai's home address, Sol's grandmother's address, and Independence Park, the site of his lessons with Coach

Anna. He'd given the agents the park address, and in mere minutes, they'd realize it. He shuddered at the thought of how they'd react, the sudden movement further irritating his wrists. *That gun-toting maniac in the driver's seat* couldn't *have been bluffing,* he thought. If regular citizens could take black life with impunity, and cops could take it with legal sanction *and* impunity on video, FBI agents could probably slit his throat on live television: impunity, legal sanction, video, and shareholder approval. The holy tetrad.

He'd almost laughed when Tilly Erickson, who he recognized from the news, had mentioned a drone strike. Atlanta wasn't Afghanistan, for chrissakes. But still, *even that* seemed plausible. He'd have to ask Apollo about drones if he ever talked to him again. He used to watch drone strike videos online all the time; he'd probably know what they were all about. *If he isn't dead,* he reminded himself. His newfound fatalism was already settling into every thought.

"You lying-ass kid!" Rick shouted as they pulled into Independence Park, parking the vehicle but letting the engine idle. Theo stared ahead, rigid with fear. His favorite Future song played from the speakers. The surrealness of the moment made Theo reflect on the car ride.

Once they'd left his house, after a stretch of angry, reckless driving, Rick had suddenly started chatting with Theo, praising his secret Tumblr, which Theo thought no one knew about, and asking him about West Coast rap. All the while, scattered Atlanta rap had been playing, ranging from deep cuts from Gangsta

Grillz mixtapes to Mike-Will-made radio fodder. Theo wasn't sure whether the guy was in too deep, using advanced interrogation techniques, or spiting Tilly Erickson, who remained silent throughout and seemed to flinch anytime they got too animated. Theo couldn't see her face, but she seemed irritated, her posture too stiff to be normal.

Familiar sounds began to pierce through Future's revelry: clicks, swooshes, beeps, eeps, flutters. Someone was going through his phone. How'd they even have his password?

"There's nothing here. We have to question him," Tilly sighed.

Theo gulped. One of her words had been a euphemism; he could feel it.

"See, this is why I hate all these new rules. Working with the phone company instead of the phone company working for us. They still haven't sent the May records!" Rick complained.

The conversation was miles above Theo's head, but he willed his every molecule to listen, seeking even the slightest hint of what was coming next.

"This drive has been a waste, but we really don't need to apprehend them today. They are on the move, but so what? It's the summer. Kids go out," Tilly said.

"But he lied. A second time. And in the back of my very comfortable vehicle, of all places. No teen is naturally that bold. Something's up."

Theo felt his bowels tighten.

"Maybe, Rick, but he's not going to budge, and I'm not going to make him. At least not in the middle of the park. What if they really are just going to do some more tags? Are we supposed to just roll up and take them in because we're pretty sure they're involved? This case can't have any weaknesses."

"If some shit goes down tonight and we didn't at least try to find out what it was, we'll have more problems than a weak case!"

Theo focused on his aching wrists. His lack of comprehension was too taxing, each gap in his understanding too bottomless to draw any conclusion but death.

"We *have* tried. We asked and he lied, and we have no more leads, so now we're waiting for the phone records to come through. If we move now, all we have is surveillance footage from a system that isn't even supposed to exist that shows them driving *near* McPherson. Even a flunky pre-law student from University of Phoenix could get that dropped."

"Tilly, we're the fucking feds! Everybody lies to us!" Rick insisted.

"We're also cybercrime specialists. Data first," Tilly calmly whispered. "Admissible data," she added.

Theo relaxed, settling into the supple leather of the back seat, relishing its softness. They needed him, desperately. He was in control. New paths began to open up, the future unfurling, death retrieving its anchor and retreating into the horizon. But the leather wasn't that soft.

If Rick and Tilly were waiting on phone records, he couldn't take the fall alone, especially if tonight's bombing happened while he was in their custody. He had to contact everyone, tell them to call it off, that their lives were at stake. He had planned on sabotaging it anyway. From the second Kai had invited him, he'd known he'd be stopping them. He couldn't bear more fires, more destruction, more guilt. He couldn't have wished for a more perfect scenario. He'd get to save his friends and repent at the same damn time. All he needed now was a phone. He had to get out of this damn Navigator.

A shrill ringtone brought him back to reality. "It's Houndum. Turn that shit off," Tilly hissed, motioning at the radio console. *Who is Houndum?* Theo wondered, listening intently as the car rattled off, Tilly's phone call immediately the only source of sound. "Yes, sir. Yes, sir. Yes, sir," Tilly fired off in different tones, her vocabulary suddenly restricted. The call ended.

"For 'safety reasons,'" Tilly began, her fingers unhappily scrunching into air quotes, "he told the fucking news that we're onto the perps." She paused. "And he gave a description of the fucking car."

"Christ, looks like we're reeling them in tonight, whether you like it or not," Rick sneered. "I'll do the honors," he announced, cracking his knuckles then stepping out of the car.

Rick opened the door, and Theo greeted him with a punishing kick to the throat, leaping out of the car and bolting into the park. Twilight stretched before him, dwindling rivulets of sunlight disintegrating into darkness. Theo scanned ahead as he dashed toward the woods. A few people were on the walking trail: a trotting older woman, a girl his age who was jogging steadily, and a duo of hulking dudes, probably football players, who were practicing sprints. He made the sensible choice.

"Ma'am, can I use your phone?" he asked as he approached the woman. She screamed and threw her phone off the path. "That works!" Theo said as he retrieved the phone without losing speed. *I should have said thank you,* he thought.

From over his shoulder he snuck a glimpse of the scene. The woman was replaced by Tilly, who was gaining on him with surprising speed. The sight of her gun rocking on her hip supercharged his resolve.

He thought of Jerry's infamous return lob as the world blurred into a single purpose. Towering conifers welcomed him into the woods on the edge of the park, where he continued his frantic pace, his legs kicking up layers of leaves and sticks. No sunlight pierced the canopy of the Georgia woods, but Theo navigated the forest nimbly, too scared to misstep. He was running so fast, he was winded after his first few steps, but a second wind would come. It had to.

He found himself on the perimeter of a junky backyard, a small plot strewn with multiple kiddie pools and a duty-knotted garden hose. Sucking down the impossibly hot air, he leaned on a short chain link fence, gasping for relief. Tilly was nowhere in sight, but Theo didn't trust the situation. The forest was too peaceful, too welcoming. Irritated, he swatted at the air, declaring his suspicion. The mosquitoes and cicadas and heat had always conspired against him. Why should they stop now?

Somewhat rested, he started to take off again, but then survival gave way to purpose, reminding him that he had messages to send. Brandishing the stolen phone, he leaped in excitement when it didn't have a password; he hadn't even considered that possibility. Crouching into a squat, he paused, struggling to remember Apollo's phone number. It seemed important to text everyone.

The memory came suddenly, a rush of numbers that felt obvious as he saw them appear on the brightly illuminated screen. "Of course," he muttered. His message was straightforward. "Hey, this is Theo! Stop the bombing. Erase the phone records. I've been caught. Love you guys! Kai the most." He hesitated before sending it. It felt too much like a farewell, too formal. He sent it anyway, immediately regretting it and sending a follow-up. "stop the bombing. erase the phone records. on the run. FBI knows everything but can't prove it or catch me. I'm Kendrick in this bitch." He laughed, wondering if his call had been picked up. Apollo had once told him about a device called Hailstorm that could surveil phones. "Hailstorm, Hailstorm, what was the range on that?" he wondered aloud, tossing the phone behind him and standing up.

"Same range as a cell tower," Tilly answered. "You move, I shoot," she decreed.

Theo froze, the darkness settling over him, unsure of where she was. She didn't sound even remotely winded, he noted.

Theo stood completely still, straining to hear Tilly's breath over the thundering symphony of his pulse, the cicadas, and cars on a nearby road.

She spoke again, her voice taunting. "You almost got away, kid, but that old lady wasn't senile. She gave us her phone number."

Theo remained quiet as she continued. "The Hailstorm cannot detect the content of phone communications, but I don't have to guess what you sent or who you sent it to. What are your friends doing tonight?"

"Bombing," Theo said, his voice faint.

"Bombing what?"

"A mural or two."

"More graffiti?"

"Like we always do."

"Of course. Get over here, kid. You're wasting my time."

Theo approached her slowly. He'd won. Abruptly, a light flashed to his left, and he felt a thud near his ribs and a ripping in his back. He yowled deeply but then felt another thud, then a rip near his lungs, curtailing his scream. He collapsed onto the forest floor, squirming, amazed at how two instances of pain could rivet his entire body. Wasn't pain supposed to be local? Footsteps approached, but Theo didn't move. The ground was cool. He liked it there.

Tilly and Rick crouched over him, their faces obscured, their bodies agitated, hot. *Why so serious?* Theo considered asking, wondering if he was clever enough to pull it off. They spoke first, their words about him but not to him. *So rude*, Theo thought.

"You shot an unarmed teen. What the fuck is your problem? Are rights just a concept to you?"

"He's a terrorist. He has no rights. Plus, he assaulted me and ran into the woods. He could have been armed."

"With what? Handcuffs?"

"It doesn't matter. Not only are we post-Tsarnaev, but the details will be classified for thirty years anyway. Back up off me, Tilly."

"He's not dead," Tilly declared, her warm fingers gliding over Theo's neck. "We need to evacuate him." Theo prayed she didn't move her hand.

Rick didn't respond. Theo imagined him crossing his arms, thinking. He seemed like a thinking man. A breeze swept over Theo's body, unnaturally cool. He didn't like it.

"We didn't mean to hurt anyone. We just wanted to have our say in the city," Theo said.

"Fuck him," Rick said, addressing Tilly. "Fuck him and all his friends. Wasting my time with graffiti. There's a war on terror going on, and these kids want to have style wars. Let's wrap this up and find his friends. "

"This won't be 'wrapped up' until we get a medevac. You should have thought of that before you shot him!"

Another thud rocked Theo's torso and exploded out of his back, the ground beneath him suddenly hot, his skin sizzling and numb all at once. He watched

Tilly stand up and dissolve into the darkness, her heat gone.

o o o

TILLY FLICKED ON HER FLASHLIGHT, SEARCHING for the stolen phone. A notification cut her search short, the phone springing to consciousness with a loud chirp. It was to her left. She retrieved it. An unlisted number had replied, "Love you too." Tilly read the three-message exchange multiple times, her eyes avoiding the boy's still body.

Rick returned with crime scene tape. Tilly shone her flashlight on the body and rolled up her sleeves, wondering if Rick had just been caught in the moment or if he had planned to shoot the kid. She didn't care enough to ask him. Their partnership worked better in silence.

Rick seemed to be on the verge of grinning as they prepared the crime scene for processing, but Tilly never caught him. She could feel his smugness though, and she accepted, definitively, that he had arranged for Sims to visit their office. It hurt to be both the target and beneficiary of so much conniving, and it was otherworldly how perfectly everything had worked out. Rick was right that they wouldn't get reprimanded for killing the kid. And he was right that they didn't really need the kid anymore. He'd ensnared his friends as soon as he'd sent that text message. *And* Rick was right that this case was whatever they made it to be. They'd known graffiti was a factor, the only factor, ever since they'd connected the J seared into the mountain to Jerry Urich, the dead kid's dead friend with a rap sheet as long as a Greek poem. But nobody would have accepted the bland truth that kids are foolish and reckless and artful, small humans with big ideas. So, Rick made the case too big to fail, too important to end with such a straightforward explanation. And she'd drank the Kool-Aid and shared the recipe, priming Houndum and the press and presumably the entire city to await a grand ending for their grand story.

Tilly felt nauseated as she climbed into Rick's Navigator, but her stomach and her thoughts settled as they left the park. Change had come.

CHAPTER 18
AUGUST 11
8:20 P.M.
92°F

KAI GNAWED AT A GAS STATION CINNAMON ROLL AS flurries of charcoal exhaust drifted past the car windshield. Liquefied sugar swished around her mouth, settling between her molars, her tongue seeking cinnamon but only finding more gooey molasses. *The rolls were on sale for a reason,* she realized as she took her last bite.

The detour down Bankhead was failing gloriously, the night's journey into the city obstructed by a gassy tractor trailer and miles of traffic. Faint traces of sunlight sputtered in the side mirror, a long kiss goodnight. Kai had thought she was doing everyone a favor by avoiding I-75/85 on the night of a Gucci concert and a Braves game, but her traffic app told her otherwise. Bankhead was backed up.

Upon receiving Theo's oblique texts, the car had become silent. Kai couldn't stop locking and unlocking her phone. Aimlessly, she scrolled through her apps, tweaking settings, changing fonts, relocating widgets, and locking the phone. Seconds later, she'd unlock her phone and the cycle would resume.

The car remained idle, and the four-wheeler's fumes remained insouciant; stasis was in the air.

Zed flicked on the radio, cracking through the silence. A deep, silky voice oozed from the speakers, sweet yet mealy, pure honeycomb. NPR, of course. Zed shrieked when she realized the content of the broadcast.

"I repeat, the license plate number is GXC6879, and the car is a black, four-door 2013 MINI Cooper. The suspects are considered armed and highly dangerous. Do not approach. I repeat—"

Zed tuned the radio to 107.9. Different voice, same news. Zed turned off the radio.

"We're fucked," Kai declared. "We can't erase phone records, and now the whole city knows our getaway car. Christ." It felt good to speak, she realized.

No one responded.

Kai regretted talking. The tetchy silence descended again. The car was wedged between two towering four-wheelers, but Kai could feel the vultures overhead, could hear the heavy wings suddenly energized by the imminence of a meal. The pillars of exhaust floating into the sky suddenly became lost opportunities for cover.

Kai found herself focusing on the sidewalk, the only place where people seemed to be moving. Each passerby drew her suspicion: a boy with a soiled

Checkers bag, an older woman with an oversized Chanel purse, two suited men, both with immaculate dreadlocks. They were all feds, she felt, her eyes trailing them through the window until they evaporated into the twilight.

Kai's mind eventually settled on the plan. It was really going down. They were going to hack more satellites and then destroy them, the ultimate tag. If they weren't caught first.

Sol opened the car door and stepped out, leaving the door ajar. Kai watched as she crouched behind the car. *What the hell was she doing?* Kai wondered, rolling down the window to peek out. Sol returned with the license plate. "Stop worrying so much," she said dryly. Kai rolled her window back up.

"Finally," Zed exhaled as the four-wheeler suddenly inched forward. The MINI followed, gliding behind it. Kai felt that they should take back roads, but she held her tongue, wary of further devaluing the clearly worthless currency that were her thoughts. After a few lights, they passed the source of all the backup: two trucks hauling giant grills had collided, face-on. Cops and emergency workers buzzed around the cleared wreckage, which was still smoking. The smell of scorched, contorted metal and sweet charred ribs was acute, assaulting the car from all sides. Images of smoldering witch cauldrons formed in Kai's mind, disparate materials forced into forbidden congress, the foulest intercourse.

"I know this is weird, but that smell makes me really hungry," Apollo confessed, speaking for the first time since Kai had gotten into the car. By the time Kai turned around to respond, he was already sunken into his laptop, his jagged widow's peak twinkling in the harsh light of the screen. Kai always wondered what kind of battery his computer used. The screen seemed excessively bright, almost confrontational. As she swiveled around to face forward, Kai saw a blip of a smile materialize on Zed's face, but it vanished just as quickly, a glitch.

The city skyline came into view, a canopy of lights and steel. Kai felt more vulnerable as adjacent vehicles disappeared down side streets. Anything seemed possible.

She glanced at her phone. Still no word from Theo. Not even an emoji. She placed the phone on silent and again rolled down the window. The noise and the air were thick and warm, like fresh grits. Kai breathed through her mouth, savoring the taste before exhaling into the night. She wished she had some bud so she could smoke it and see her breath as it floated away. Zed rolled down the remaining windows.

Bankhead terminated at Northside Drive. Zed tapped her fingers on the wheel as they waited for the light. Kai hummed along.

"Left?" Zed asked.

"Left," Kai confirmed.

"Thanks," Zed replied.

Kai was surprised when she continued talking.

"Hey, I know where we are! This is the backside of Tech!"

"Yeah, it is," Kai said. "Right on Tenth."

The MINI eased onto Tenth Street, cutting through Georgia Tech's campus. The campus was a little bland, Kai thought. Apollo and Zed could have done better. But ever since they'd gone to orientation, Apollo and Zed had seemed ambivalent about attending, so she didn't mention it. And Sol wasn't going anywhere. Kai wasn't sure what that meant, but her mom had implied it was some sort of tragedy; Kai felt bad when she realized she didn't disagree.

Kai's phone received a call as they crossed over Williams Street. The designated image for Theo's number blinked the screen awake. The picture was a selfie they'd taken on Good Friday. Theo had insisted they listen to Kanye West all day, and she had obliged, but only on the condition that they take a selfie mimicking Kanye at his angriest. It took fifteen minutes of snapping and seven minutes of editing to find the correct combination of disdain and ego, but this picture was the one. Their jaws were rigidly square, their eyes scornful. Kai loved the theatricality of it. They could never be that upset with anything, especially when they were together.

"You can start looking for parking," Kai might have heard Sol say. Her voice was obstructed by the hot phone pressed against Kai's left ear.

"Hello? Are you okay?"

"I'm perfectly fine, thank you," Rick said.

"Who is this? You're not Theo."

"I'm not. I'm Rick Herrington, an FBI agent. Theo's dead, I'm afraid."

"Fuck you."

"I have no reason to lie to you, young lady."

"Fuck you!" Kai shouted as Zed eased into an on-street parking spot on Peachtree Place.

"Ahhh, let it out. It is hard news, I understand."

Tears began to dangle from Kai's chin. She felt slighted when she realized she hadn't even felt them slide down her cheeks.

"What do you want?" she whispered, hoping she was being conned.

"I want to bargain. You turn yourselves in, I don't have any more dead teenagers in my case report."

"Any more" echoed in Kai's head. He'd said it so casually.

"And what if I refuse?" Kai asked, putting the phone on speaker mode. Her ear was burning.

"Well, Kaila, I think we both know you're not stupid enough to do that. Not only do I know where you just parked off of Spring Street, I know where you're going, and I have a pretty good idea of what you're going to do. It's not happening. I've had Google Atlanta completely evacuated, Atlanta's finest are on the way as we speak, and all military satellites have been moved from Atlanta airspace. This is over, children. I know you thought you could evade us with your firewalls and data encryptions and IP blocking, but this is the big time. We've got phone records. You should have stuck with spray paint and ink pens."

"Bye, nigga," Apollo blared from the back seat, reaching over the console and grabbing Kai's phone. He ended the call, then tossed the phone onto the street, where it was quickly devoured by oncoming traffic. Kai wished they had used burners like the first time.

They got out of the car and headed toward the building. After a few steps, Zed's phone rang.

It was "Theo" again. Zed sighed and lobbed her phone into the street. It tarried before being overrun by a herd of vehicles, the lit phone a dull ember on the jet-black asphalt. Apollo's phone lit up soon after. He threw it directly at a passing car, striking a passenger in the face through an open window. They all laughed at once, deep laughs that penetrated the noise of the city. Kai was glad they were on a one-way street.

"Do we have to do this?" Kai asked as they idled on the sidewalk. "Is it really our job to destroy these satellites? Theo is dead."

Sol kept walking. Then her phone rang, loud and shrill and funky. The ringtone was "My Summer Vacation," by Ice Cube. In April, Theo had insisted that she both obtain the song and make it his ringtone. Kai was surprised that Sol had obliged.

Sol answered her phone with a bark. "What?"

Rick was loud, emboldened. "Last chance, kiddies. It's 2019. Cops show up, someone tends to get shot."

"Well, I guess you've got plenty of reason to stay the fuck away from us."

"I'm not a cop," Rick said. The call ended.

o o o

TILLY STUDIED RICK'S FACE AS THEY FLEW DOWN Peachtree, a detachable light flickering on the roof. He seemed thrilled. This would be their first time hauling in perps in the middle of a crime. They usually cuffed people when they were fiddling with their Keurigs or changing the cat litter. Rick liked to call those kinds of pickups *data dumps*: show up and unload the evidence, smothering the perp all at once, like pouring ashes into a fire. It was the most reliable way to bring in perps. It was natural for people to resist some mudslinging, but being buried alive brought swift acquiescence. *Kill Bill: Vol. 2* was a fantasy. This case was different, though. This was a hunt.

Midtown was active. Cars were reluctant to pull aside, pedestrians made their own crosswalks, Uber drivers loitered near the curbs of restaurants. Tilly hadn't been out all summer, she realized as they passed the Vortex. The last guy she'd dated had taken her to an open mic comedy show there in early May. She'd been struck by how many variations of bearded white man there were. The jokes weren't as variable. Dicks, self-derision, anxiety about gentrification, comments on unique romantic experiences that were actually quite common: it all had reminded her of the internet.

Her phone rang. It was the captain of the two precincts helping them with the arrests.

"What?" Tilly huffed. "Are you fucking serious?" she screamed, spiking the phone onto the car floor.

Rick looked over at her as they waited at a light, somehow still thrilled. A homeless woman skipped across the street. Tilly found it unsettling. She remained silent until the car started moving again, turning left onto Tenth.

"So?" he asked.

"The officers we were supposed to be given are being rerouted to State Farm Arena. There was a technical mishap at the Gucci concert. People are panicking."

"Don't they understand that the goddamn city's at stake?"

"I don't know what Houndum told them, Rick. But maybe this is actually what we need? These are just kids, after all. Why are we sending a SWAT team after them? Two of them visited a college last month. They can't be doing anything too radical."

Rick parked the SUV on the sidewalk, dropping his voice to a murmur as he checked his ammunition. "Tilly, this isn't an investigation anymore. The kid said the word 'bombing.' You've seen the images from the Rudolph bombings; you don't want that much blood on your hands. We don't have to ask any further questions. We just have to go pick these kids up." He paused, calculating. "If you're feeling squeamish about it, I can go alone. I will have to put that in the report, though."

Tilly scowled at him, disgusted at how much power he had amassed simply from claiming he had power. In a single day, he'd rewritten their job description a dozen times. They'd gone from cybercrime investigators to bounty hunters. And the bounty wasn't even necessarily tangible; it was prestige, privilege, glory. Meager reward for a child's life, Tilly felt. Still, she found herself stepping into the heat of the night, armed and even exhilarated. The case really was coming to a close, she realized.

The lobby of Google Atlanta was more austere than Tilly expected. It looked, quite simply, like a lobby: chairs, a desk, home improvement magazines, company insignia, a sleek coffee machine, a water cooler. She had anticipated Android tablets dangling from the ceilings, perpetually burning effigies of Steve Jobs, Roombas slavishly cleaning the floors, a self-driving car practicing three-point turns. Instead she found white walls accented with splashes of green, red, blue, and yellow. "Corporations gonna corporate," she imagined the old Rick saying, if she, the old Tilly, had confessed her surprise. Instead, she said nothing and followed him as he stalked toward the stairs, providing cover as they walked through the open atrium of the ground floor.

A sleek card reader hugged the doorway to the stairs, but made no fuss as Rick twisted the handle and nudged the door forward. Tilly knew from her days as a security auditor that automated access points were notoriously unreliable, but she told herself that these kids were responsible for the easy entry. She needed to be prepared for whatever happened next.

"We're gonna have to split up," Rick announced, holstering his gun.

"Why?" Tilly asked, gun still in hand, gripped.

"Google agreed to evacuate but they wouldn't confirm or deny that they have a supercomputer on the premises. It could be in the basement, could be in a lab, could be that gorgeous coffee machine in the lobby. They wouldn't budge."

"Fucking techholes."

"Honestly, I can't even blame them," Rick said as he ascended the stairs. "We're the FBI. You don't want us to know your secrets."

Tilly shrugged and headed downstairs. It took her three full flights to reach an exit, but there was only one floor awaiting her. Cautiously, she stepped through a door and into a narrow hallway with a towering ceiling. It felt as if she were in a silo for a giant paper plane.

Motion-sensing lights incrementally illuminated the corridor, a new pair of bulbs bolting awake each time Tilly stepped forward. The wall on her right was made entirely of thick, translucent glass, but no doors were in sight. Tilly gripped her gun tighter.

As she began to approach the end of the hall, a door finally became visible, twenty yards ahead on her right, opening into the room behind the glass wall. Tilly slowed to a prowl as she approached it, her body taut. Calmly, she tested the knob. It was open. She immediately burst inside.

She found herself standing on immaculate hardwood floors, the sweet-sour smell of stale sweat wafting through her nostrils. No one was in sight. Tilly laughed, holstering her gun and admiring the fact that she was standing in a fully-stocked gymnasium. Basketballs, towels, and unfinished water bottles littered the floor, but even that small untidiness was impressive. *At the time the building was ordered to be evacuated, people had been* playing basketball at work, she thought. "I don't even play basketball when I'm *not* working," she said aloud, her tone both mocking and mournful. She picked up a basketball and held it, awash in memories of high school: unplanned leisure, AOL Instant Messenger, jump shots.

She returned to the stairwell, ascending slowly. Finding the door to the fourth floor ajar, she stepped forward cautiously. A muffled gunshot rang out. "Shit!" Tilly shouted, brandishing her gun and crouching. *Was Rick okay?* she wondered as she found cover behind a work desk cluttered with paperwork. Hearing no other gunshots, Tilly rose and followed the faint sound of voices. Ducking into a hallway, she slowed to a tiptoe as the voices grew louder. Another gunshot sounded off, followed by screams.

Tilly stopped at the edge of an open door, pressing her back against an adjacent wall, listening.

"Guys, we don't have to do this. What are we still doing here?" Kai asked.

"You can leave if you want, but a nigga literally just got shot, so I'm doing what the fuck I came here to do while I can do it," Sol insisted.

"*You* are not doing a damn thing," Apollo responded. "Me and Zed are the ones who are entering the long and lat coordinates, and we're the ones who programmed the lockpick. Chill out."

"I don't take orders from you, Apollo. Don't forget about these."

An object flew through the air, landing flatly on a hand. Tilly guessed it was a notebook of some kind, maybe a phone.

"Sol, we've already talked about this. We're not going to shoot at houses. We're here to hit other satellites, nothing else. Nothing has changed," Zed affirmed.

"I'm sorry. Apollo and I have an arrangement," Sol said.

The talking suddenly stopped. Something was missing, Tilly felt. *Where the hell is Rick?* she wondered. And who had the damn gun? Was she just paranoid?

"You don't control me just because you point a gun at me," Apollo said coolly.

"Shit," Tilly mouthed, breathing nervously. One of them was armed. She considered her options. She could take them by surprise. She could try to negotiate with them. She could retreat and call for backup. She could flee. None of the options thrilled her, especially without knowing Rick's status, but she had to move now, before things escalated further.

She decided to check on Rick. "Rick, are you alive?" she shouted over her left shoulder, revealing herself.

"Yeah, they've got my gun," he yelped back, his voice curt.

"Kids, I know that you have no reason to trust me after what he's done, but please return his gun to me. I promise that I will not harm you."

No one responded, not even Rick.

Tilly spoke again. "I'm going to kick my gun across the doorway, disarming myself. Please do the same."

"Jesus Christ, Tilly, just come in here and fucking shoot them. I'm fucking dying in here!" Rick hissed.

Tilly paused. Maybe Rick was right. What was she doing? Every bullet in her clip was backed and approved by the entire federal government. A legion of judges, secretaries, bailiffs, senators, congressional aides, and analysts had authorized these bullets to take any path she chose, any trajectory she willed. She had a license to kill and a warrant to do it at her discretion. Why was she hesitating?

She sucked in a deep breath, harboring the air in her chest, relishing its presence even as it transformed into an absence, a vacuum of unwanted gas.

Exhaling, she pivoted into a crouch, positioning herself in the center of the open doorway. Rick had lied again, she realized too late, diving forward as bullets sped past her, one acquiring a chunk of her left ear. On her belly, she fired back twice, both bullets striking Rick in his neck, toppling him over.

Tilly rose slowly, advancing toward Rick's shaking body. His gun hung limply from contorted fingers. Tilly kicked it toward the doorway, holstering her own gun. Silently, she examined him. He was still alive, but he seemed to be frozen in an eternity of pain. His entire face was a grimace, every crevice broadcasting some unspeakable distress. Tilly stared directly at him as his body began to violently shake, blood fleeing his wounds. He didn't look back at her.

Bending down, Tilly closed his eyelids and turned to the kids, who were huddled together in a corner. One of them was bleeding, but he was quiet. "What happened here?" she asked calmly.

Kai immediately spoke. "He ambushed us while we were in the middle of bombing. Apollo's dumb ass said he'd rather die, and Rick shot him in the arm." She stopped talking to glare at Apollo. "He then told us to continue what we were doing. He said that he 'had to make us worthy.'"

Tilly didn't reply. She knew exactly what "worthy" meant. He was going to make them carry out their plan and then kill them. He was making the case news-ready, promotion-ready, politically sound, flattening their motives. She'd underestimated the thoroughness of his ambition.

Troubled, she wondered about her own ambitions. Saving these kids? Getting a promotion? Saving the city? She felt disappointed. Her ambitions were all obligations. How motherly.

"How far along did you guys get?" Tilly inquired, finally taking the time to examine the room. It felt like a temple. The floors and the walls were a shiny white marble, their surfaces so clean that the lights nested in the floor seemed to beam from all directions, like a disco ball turned outside in. A CPU in the shape of a sphere hung from the ceiling, floating over a circular table where small fans provided it with a constant breeze. Adjacent to those fans were keyboards and monitors. Tilly felt like she was at the center of a star system.

"We destroyed seventeen out of the forty-four satellites we were aware of," Zed declared, her voice flat, but proud.

Tilly felt relieved. "Well, assuming that no one is hurt from satellite debris and no communications satellites are damaged, that's a pretty victimless crime. You didn't hear this from me, but with the right lawyer, you guys might get off pretty easily. Vandalism is still vandalism."

"Perhaps. But we also fired at the Georgia Dome. And Centennial Olympic Park. And Atlantic Station. And SunTrust Park. And Emory. And Municipal Market. And the streetcar. And about half of Buckhead." Apollo paused. "And two random houses that Sol forced on me," he added with a smug scowl.

"*We*?" Zed shrieked into Apollo's face. "*We* agreed to destroy the satellites. *We* did the hard work of tracking down the satellite orbits. *We* programmed the digital lockpick. *We* all came here together to do the same thing. To honor Jerry. You…you have done something else. You have taken our futures from us."

"At least you have a future," Sol jeered.

"Cut the shit, Sol," Kai squawked. "You know your parents have nothing on you. They're just trying to shake you down because they think they can."

"Her parents probably don't even have a life," Apollo chuckled.

"*I* don't have a life," Zed asserted, shoving Apollo into a wall. He looked away as she repeatedly jabbed her finger into his shoulder. "We could have gotten away with this, could have gone to school, could have done something, but now this moment will define us forever. Did you think to ask me about how I felt? Did you think about anyone but yourself? Did you think at all? You killed people!"

"Even if some good ones die, fuck it, the Lord'll sort 'em," Apollo rapped.

"Fuck you, Apollo. You don't even believe in God," Kai spewed.

Tilly listened to their exchange, her head spinning, her body stiff with disbelief. The slab of ear she'd lost must have distorted something, she speculated. That self-assured look on Apollo's face was teenage arrogance, not truth. He couldn't have just committed mass murder. He couldn't have just razed his hometown. He was trolling her. That's what kids did online these days, wasn't it? Especially guys. Even black guys? Probably. It was a new day. Niggas had been in Paris since 2011. Maybe they were on 4chan too. She didn't tweet as much as she used to. She still logged into Myspace when she had a little too much Chardonnay. Things were different now.

When she was coming of age, trolling was like white guys' new national pastime. She'd read an academic study on it somewhere, for some case. Something about privilege and power. The most privileged tended to use power the most flippantly because they knew they would never lose it. That's why Eminem was so extra. Teenagers, all teenagers, thought of themselves as almighty. He was just being a teenager, that was it. "Teenagers gonna teenage," old Rick might have said.

Tilly gawked at his motionless body, stroking the part of her maimed ear that was left intact. The pond of blood around him accented the white room. *Is this how bears would decorate if they had human rugs?* Tilly wondered. That was a question old Rick might have asked. Was it old Rick or new Rick that she'd shot?

Could she have shot him in the legs? She'd never killed a coworker before. Was she the same Tilly?

Tired of posing so many questions to herself, Tilly turned to Apollo, who was crouched in a corner, his arms being wrapped in T-shirt tourniquets by Zed. "Why?"

"Why what?"

"Why do all this?"

"Because Black lives matter."

"I'm not your Facebook friend, kid. I've been through your search history. The first time you Googled Black Lives Matter was in August. And you didn't even click any links. Give me a real answer."

"Black privacy matters."

"I'm still not convinced."

"Well, that's on you. You took the internet away from me."

"I'm not the NSA, kid. I'm FBI. And they took it from me, too. I used to be a hacker. It was never the glorious life you probably think it is, full of ideological purity and utopian ideals. Ascetics don't have friends."

"You killed my friend. And my friends are only my friends because their friend got killed by you."

"I'm not your fucking friend, you maniac," Kai interjected.

Sol laughed, drawing Tilly's attention. "Why did you do all this?" Tilly asked her. Sol laughed again, somehow above the entire situation. Tilly envied her.

"My partner killed your friend," Tilly said, appealing to Kai, who seemed to be the most worked up. "I've never killed anyone who wasn't trying to kill me."

Zed finally spoke up. "What a great standard," she scoffed.

"Yeah, it's kept me alive and stopped me from shooting innocents, unlike my partner."

"You are your partner," Apollo muttered.

"My partner's dead, and you would be too if I hadn't saved your smug ass. Those holes in your arm would have been in your chest when he was done with you. And your smart-ass mouth."

"If you wanted to save me, you would have killed yourself."

Tilly didn't respond. She wasn't paid enough to tolerate snark from teenagers, especially sociopathic nihilist teenagers who trolled her with lies about leveling their hometowns. He'd probably just put on a light show. Houndum hadn't even called her to yell. The kid was definitely lying. He'd just been given the address of Sol's parents. She'd caught them midway. There was no way he'd struck all these places while his friends and Rick were watching. Something was amiss.

A city erupting into chaos couldn't be this quiet, she felt. Irritated, she fished through her pockets for plastic zip ties, tossing a few pairs over Rick's dead body. They landed at Kai's feet.

"Put those on," she commanded, opening her blazer to flash her gun. Kai and Zed obliged immediately.

"I'm not leaving here in handcuffs," Sol said coolly.

"Stretchers are also available, as well as body bags," Tilly sneered, grabbing her gun and using it to wave at the remaining cuffs. Sol finally obliged, turning to help Apollo shackle himself before cuffing herself.

Tilly led them out of the room in single file, stopping to retrieve Rick's gun and gesturing for the teens to pass. The gun was still hot.

Bringing up the rear, Tilly directed them to the stairwell, walking carefully as they descended in silence. Tilly winced with every step, cupping her ear and hoping its missing fragment could be salvaged by CSI. Midway down the final flight, a tremor rocked the building, sending Tilly face-first into the banister, followed by a sharp tumble down the stairway. Headfirst, she landed at the bottom of the steps, her body lying limp as she drifted into unconsciousness, blackness moving across the edges of her vision like a flame on a fuse.

CHAPTER 19
AUGUST 11
10:32 P.M.
98°F

H*OTLANTA WAS FINALLY AN APPROPRIATE NAME*, A*POLLO* thought, swinging his dangling feet over a charred Honda Civic that he'd repurposed as a throne. The street was empty, devoid of traffic and life. Apollo sat calmly as giant flames snaked around buildings, producing spires of smoke that choked the sky, Towers of Babel spreading the new universal language of rebirth and revolution.

He'd really burned it all down. All the bullshit. All the corporatism. All the opportunism. All the wires and wiretaps. Welcome to Atlanta.

Zed was a fool to choose college over this, a true future, one with possibilities that they could imagine and build rather than apply for, drive to, tweet about, smoke away. How could she have left him so decisively, so easily? Her, Kai, Sol. They'd all bonded over the past month, discussing the future. They'd all been scared, he felt, their eyes lowering and glazing over when they thought about majors, classes, responsibility, bills. The only thing they looked forward to was the plan. Apollo had seen it. It was their only freedom.

And he had seized it. The tags didn't have to be an ode to Jerry or a final act of defiance before settling down. This could be the moment they unsettled, drowning in the radical openness of authentic liberation. They could have become true celestials, gods of the cosmos, stewards of change. Yet they settled right back into their fears the moment he gave them an out. So wormlike. He felt betrayed.

How could she have done this to him? She said she loved him, but here he was, alone. Why had it been so easy for her to choose? Why had she looked at him like he'd double-crossed her? He wasn't Theo. He wasn't a flirt. He'd given her exactly what she'd wanted, what she'd asked for. Right there in the back seat, just how she liked it.

Apollo stared into the pillar of fire engulfing the skyscraper across the street, recalling his last moment in her presence. There Zed was, dragging the FBI agent out into the street as the building collapsed like a dream. The woman was at least forty pounds heavier than her, but she summoned the strength to carry her, cradling her gashed head like a newborn and laying her down on a patch of grass. Then she was gone, Kai and Sol at her side, their plastic handcuffs cut loose with a jagged shard of glass, the agent slung over Sol's shoulder. Why did she have to be so goddamn noble?

That woman was authorized by a government that didn't exist anymore.

The revolution was fucking lonely. He wished Theo was here. Was he really dead? He had to be. This had all been done in his name. Jerry's story was moving, but it had been Theo who was the true inspiration. He had carried out his plan and been broken by it, losing Kai, his center, his way. Apollo was still whole. As his plan germinated, he'd felt himself become complete, felt his body become definite, concrete.

This must be how Zed felt when she brought her sketches to life, repossessing those privatized slabs of the city and releasing them back to the public.

Perhaps. But this was so much more than repossession, Apollo felt. This wasn't guerilla eminent domain, piecemeal seizure. He hadn't taken the city back; he had hacked it, cutting a hole in the fences of enclosure and watching the source code bleed into the ether. Today was the day Dixie died. Again.

Apollo soaked in the crackling hum of fire consuming metal, his hand gliding over his cheeks as he wiped away the latest wave of nervous, triumphant sweat. *Theo couldn't have handled this heat,* Apollo assured himself, laughing out loud despite the globules of tears forming in his eyes.

How had Theo died? he wondered. A bullet was the culprit, he knew, but where had it struck? Did Theo fire shots of his own? Was it an execution or a fight? A struggle or a surrender? Had it been planned from the moment they'd met him, or had it just happened on the fly, a death made from scratch? The only person who knew was Tilly. He'd have to find her, ask her about Theo's last moments, if he could even muster speaking to her. She was vermin, a vestige of an outdated order. It was infuriating that she was somewhere in his city, breathing the air that mere hours ago she had clogged with surveillance and oversight. Zed, Kai, and Sol could find their way as they saw fit, but Tilly had already chosen her path, and in a world of freedom, it had to be closed off.

Apollo leaped from the car, shuddering as a splitting pain shot through his knee. He should have given them a little more time to escape the building. Finding his bearings, he headed down Tenth Street, toward the highway. The streets glowed in the light of the ambient flames. Emptied cars littered the road, some crushed by falling debris. Bodies, some moving, some still, were just as common, but Apollo strolled past them, amazed by the views. It was unfathomable how wide the laser had been. A house-sized hole had been punched right through Google Atlanta, pulverizing the street. Apollo slid down into a crater the size of a pool, gleefully kicking rocks as he made his way to its center. If his hands hadn't still been handcuffed, he would have thrown a fist into the air, signing his beautiful work.

After a strained climb out of the other side of the crater, he reached the Tenth Street Bridge, turning around to admire his work from afar. Smoke continued to pour into the sky, but the sound of the fires was muted by some odd drone. Apollo peered over the edge of the bridge. There was traffic! Cars, SUVs, buses, trucks floating along with no particular urgency.

He seethed. How had he not thought to strike the highways? Even those shortsighted Black Lives Matter activists had known to target the highway. He felt like an imbecile. All that planning undermined by one forgotten target. If only Kai and Sol and Zed could have been trusted to help him. They would have thought of this. He resented them for forcing him to take on the burden of liberation by himself. He turned back to his flames, oranges and yellows and reds feeding on the steely bones of the city in an orgiastic frenzy. The heat of the fires was still tremendous, grazing Apollo's skin, but it suddenly seemed bland, stale, pedestrian.

A slow-moving shape on Tenth Street caught Apollo's eye. The shape walked casually, almost leisurely, shoulders flowing forward, legs swinging. *Yes*, Apollo thought, *there are already converts.* He stood still, eager to meet this new comrade, already enamored with his clear familiarity.

"Nigga, what the fuck are you still doing here?" Sol belted as she stepped from the shadows and into the firelight.

"What are you doing here?" Apollo parroted back.

"I'm here to get Zed's car."

"Why?"

"To get the fuck out of here, obviously!"

"There's nothing to run from. I've been out here for an hour since you cowards left me, and I haven't heard a single siren."

Sol inhaled deeply. "Apollo, as I've always told you, you're a fucking idiot. We were supposed to sabotage a satellite system. You *attacked* a city. Tanks, drones, or whatever they're sending for you don't have sirens."

"I didn't attack the city. I liberated it."

"I don't know what you thought you were doing in the back seat, but this is not liberation. This is you being an asshole."

"You're one to judge. You made me kill your parents and your cousin."

"My parents were at work, and my cousin was at Bible study. I wanted you to hit their houses. Very big difference."

"Wait, what? But you hate them. You hate everything they stand for."

"So? Nigga, I also hate Iggy Azalea and *Housewives of Atlanta* and cheesecake. I haven't killed anybody over it, though."

"I don't need your condescension. Where's Zed and Kai and Tilly?"

Sol paused. "They're making some phone calls, trying to fix this fucking mess you made."

"You snitching assholes! Not only is there nothing to fix, but snitching won't help you. We all made this mess, not just me. What did you think the logical conclusion of hijacking government satellites was?"

"Honestly, I trusted you. I didn't think we'd get caught because you wouldn't let us. And if we did, I was thinking we'd get locked up, get the Pussy Riot treatment, then get released. What the hell did *you* expect from all of this?"

Apollo opened his mouth to speak before he realized the question was rhetorical.

Sol continued. "Did you fail geography or something? You attacked a city while you were in it. Jesus!" Sol turned back toward the shadow engulfing the side of the bridge where she'd come from, her voice dropping to a harsh deadpan. "Dude, a few weeks ago, it really seemed like you were done with that childish shit, always picking conviction over compromise. But look at this shit." Her arm shot up into the air, gesturing at nothing, everything.

"It's beautiful."

"That's the problem, Apollo. Revolution is supposed to be hideous. Only ideals are beautiful."

Sol sauntered off toward the conflagration as swaggeringly as she came, leaving Apollo on the bridge, his skin aglow in the light of the growing flames. Undisturbed, traffic continued underneath, a calm chaos of light and speed and friction. Minutes later, Zed's MINI burst onto the bridge, cruising away from the fires. Apollo watched as the taillights slowly evaporated into the darkness, swallowed whole by the maw of the night.

AUTHOR'S ACKNOWLEDGMENTS

I had a lot of help. In a broad sense, I'm forever indebted to Mom, Dad, Jr., Nadine, Mike, Tommee, Torrence, Cedric, Cameron, and Hannah. Y'all fed me and made me laugh and gave me *that look* when I was mouthing off. More specifically, I thank Harold for reading the earliest drafts chapter by chapter and patiently offering writing tips and additional reading. I thank Kelly for giving me constant encouragement and providing critical insights about the business of publishing. Shouts to Hafidha for emphasizing perspective and tone. Props to ZR for pointing me toward writing resources and highlighting places where the narrative could be strengthened. *Preesh*, Sheldon, for reading so many versions of the manuscript that you could probably invoice me (please don't). And finally, thank you Rashele and Luna for lovingly insisting that I go to sleep and take walks and chill out; it was always good advice. You learn a lot writing a book, but my main lesson has been that I'm damn lucky to know so many brilliant and generous people.

My fortune extends to my reception by Vanessa and the rest of the Kindred Books and Brain Mill Press staff. When my manuscript sat on my Google Drive, I was simply pleased with it; through your efforts, I've adopted a swelling pride. Thank you.

ABOUT *THE* AUTHOR

Stephen Kearse is a reporter and critic from Atlanta. He now lives in Washington, DC, where he regularly laments the lack of good biscuits. He has been published by the *New York Times Magazine*, *Hazlitt*, *Pitchfork*, and *The Ringer*, among other outlets. He loves Georgia summers.